# Pretend Best Friends

—

# Girls in Motion

Natasja Eby

ISBN-13: 978-1738872916

The characters and events portrayed in this book are fictitious. Any similarity to real persons, living or dead, is coincidental and not intended by the author. Should you find yourself inhabiting the body of another person, please seek medical attention immediately.

Cover and book design by Natasja Eby

Published by Natasja Eby
https://www.natasjaeby.com/

# DEDICATION

For Tracy, Laryssa, and Marlene (and Isla).
And for Shadow, a very good boy.

# ACKNOWLEDGMENTS

To the fans of this series.
Thank you for continuing to read these books even though you know what will happen at the end. You're all the best! Please thank my amazing editor for making my writing sparkle.

# Chapter One

Sam slowed his gait to match Tony's uneven one. If Tony didn't have his nose in his notebook, it wouldn't have been so bad. As it was, Sam's arms were full of shopping bags, so he couldn't even guide Tony if he wanted to. The shopping mall was crowded, what with it being Sunday afternoon, and Sam had spent every last dime he had on his special outfits. Now all he wanted was to get home.

"Wait..." Tony stopped, prompting a repressed sigh from Sam. "What did I even write? Because the last thing I said was—" He flipped a few pages back.

Tapping his foot impatiently, Sam said, "'The beast's clawed foot inched closer to Valentino's terrified eyes. And then—'"

"Ohhhhh, yes." Tony started on his path again and now it was Sam trying to keep up. "Right, and then Valentino reaches for his sword. Somehow..."

Sam chuckled. Tony liked books way too much for Sam's tastes. And when he was focused on his stories, he was a bit of a space case. But Sam wouldn't trade his friendship with Tony for the world. After all, Tony had spent hours upon hours helping Sam improve his reading, writing, and comprehension skills. Without Tony, Sam would have definitely been held back a year and probably would have no friends.

And without Sam, Tony would be walking into every single shopper in his vicinity. Not only was Sam making a way through the crowds with his tall stature, broad shoulders, and commanding presence, but he also kept nudging Tony in the right direction.

Tony was always like this though. If he weren't staring at his notebook, he was reading a book, and if not that, it was his phone. But Sam didn't mind. After all, who else would spend a whole day at the mall with Sam to buy three entirely new outfits just to impress some modeling scouts? Certainly not his older brother, Ty. Maybe Tony's sisters, Maddy and Stella, but Sam wasn't desperate enough to ask them.

"Yeah," Sam said, wondering how Tony would write himself out of a plot hole—again. "Somehow. Maybe he uses the force."

Tony flicked a glance at him. "I can't steal someone else's intellectual property, Sunny."

"It was a joke, dude."

"Oh."

Shaking his head, Sam managed to nudge Tony to the side. There was a beautiful water fountain in the middle of the main hall, flanked by benches, and Sam needed to set his stuff down for a second. Tony sat on an empty bench, his gaze never leaving his notebook.

"Are you going to finish this scene before Saturday?" Sam said. "Or are you going to bail on this reading like last time?"

Tony closed his eyes and tried to imagine himself reading his own writing to a crowd of people. Nope. Even in his imagination, it was terrifying. He shook his head.

"Still?" Sam put his bags down next to Tony. "Come on, man, you have to let people read it eventually."

Tony opened his eyes again to give Sam a wary look. "Letting them read it and reading it to them are very different things."

"Sure." There was no arguing with Tony. He thought of every possibility. Sam reached into his back pocket, which he realized was alarmingly empty. "Oh, shoot, dude. I totally left my wallet at the last store."

"Go," Tony said, gesturing with his pencil. "I'll watch your stuff."

"Will you, though?"

Tony looked up and gave him a placid smile. "Yes. Go."

As Sam rushed away, Tony looked back down at his chicken scratch. Should he try to be clearer when he was writing? Probably. But he had neither the time nor the ambition to improve his handwriting. He was too busy trying to improve his storytelling.

Someone rushed past him, rustling the pages of his notebook. He looked up with a scowl only to find Ana Dellagusta wildly swinging a baseball bat around. Okay, so it wasn't quite wild. In fact, she looked like she was in total control, but she was also in the middle of a busy mall.

"Ana," Tony said in his nicest voice. When she kept swinging, he spoke louder. No dice.

Putting his pencil in his notebook to keep his spot, he wrapped the elastic around it, and then rose. He went over to Ana, narrowly avoiding getting hit. The bat came straight for his head, and he caught it with his free hand. Now he had Ana's attention.

"Ugh, what do you want?" She tried pulling her bat away, but Tony held it tightly.

"I want you to stop acting crazy. You almost hit me."

"You're in my way, Cleaver," Ana said.

Tony rolled his eyes and pushed the bat lightly towards her. "Stop swinging your bat around, Dellagusta."

"First of all—" she lowered her bat and held a finger up "—nice accent. Second, make me."

"*Make me?*" Tony scowled. "What are you, five? Just stop doing that, you're being annoying."

Ana lifted her bat and, with incredible accuracy, tapped Tony's notebook straight out of his hands. While shouting at her, he flailed around trying to catch it. However, he knocked it midair and it fell into the fountain.

"*Ana!*"

"I'm so sorry," Ana said quickly, her bright brown eyes now wide. She dropped the bat and leaned over the side of the fountain, reaching for the book.

"Don't touch it!" he snarked. "Haven't you done enough?"

"I'm trying to help."

He tried to shoulder her out of the way, but she was surprisingly sturdy and steady on her feet. "You'll just wreck it even more. Get away!"

The book was now out of his reach and it bobbed up and down in the rippling fountain. With no amount of irritation, he saw Ana's bat reach into the water. Ana expertly fished the book out and flipped it towards Tony. He choked back a sob as he gently opened the pages to assess the damage.

"I'm so s—"

"*Don't,*" Tony said, cutting off what he was sure was Ana's pathetic attempt at an apology. Holding the book over the fountain's edge, he let as much water drip out of it as possible. "You're not sorry. Don't say it."

She stepped closer, holding a hand out. "But I am!"

"Stop." He turned around, realizing he'd left the shopping bags all alone on the bench when he'd told Sam he'd watch them. "Sam's stuff! I have to watch Sam's stuff. Where even is he?"

Sam, meanwhile, had tried rushing his way through the mall, desperate to get his wallet back. But the crowds were too thick. Maybe they didn't have

4

anywhere to be, but he did.

Sam was no football player like his brother. If he worked out more, he'd have the right physique for it. He could cut through a crowd in a slow, meandering way. But if he were Ty, he'd be unapologetically shoving these people out of the way. Oh, what he wouldn't do to have Ty here, instead of having left all his bags with his very scatterbrained best friend.

As it was, Sam was squeezing past people, apologizing repeatedly but also in an irritated way to get past them. He tapped on shoulders, slid past families with little kids, and skirted around a man in a motorized scooter. He'd almost reached the last store he'd gone to when he bumped full-on into someone else. Fortunately, he caught her by wrapping an arm around her waist.

*Unfortunately*, it was Valerie Davis, the ice queen of Bridgetown High.

"Sorry," he said quickly.

"You are *not*," she snipped as she forcefully pushed his arm away. "What are you rushing around like that for anyway? Don't you have any decorum? Seriously, Samuel, why do you have to take up so much space?" She looked him up and down with clear disdain in her dark brown eyes.

"I do *not* take up so much space!" he retorted hotly. "You make me sound like an elephant. Give me a break, Valerie."

"Give *you* a break?" She crossed her arms and scoffed. "Like you need any more breaks in life."

"I don't—" He was going to say he didn't even know where to start to correct her perception of his life. But then he remembered his wallet. "I don't have time for this. Bye!"

He whirled around and continued on his frantic path. When a taloned hand grasped his arm, he suppressed a sigh. If she was going to hold on, she'd better be able to keep up. Curling his arm in, he almost pulled her down.

"You think you can just walk away from me?" Valerie said as she did, indeed, keep pace with him.

"Look, I'm really busy, so if you could just—" He shook his arm to get rid of her, but she held on tight. "I seriously need to get to this store, Val. Let me *go*."

"Oh, no," she said sarcastically as they approached the store's open doorway. "What will happen if you can't get your shop on?"

Shaking his head, he ignored her and strode up to the checkout. There was a line waiting, but he cut in front of the next person and slapped his hand down on the counter.

"I left a wallet here a while ago," he said hastily to the wide-eyed clerk. "Like, maybe twenty minutes ago? Please tell me it's still here."

"Uhhh…" The clerk looked past him and then down at the counter. "Let me check…"

"Sam, you're being *so* rude," Val said, gesturing to the others waiting more or less patiently.

"What does it look like?" the clerk, whose head had disappeared behind the counter, asked.

Ignoring Val, Sam said, "It's brown Italian leather monogrammed with the letters *S D* on it. Is it there?"

"Yup!" The clerk popped back up and, with a tight smile, held out the wallet.

"Thank you *so* much," Sam said as he grabbed it. Letting out a sigh of relief, he turned to the waiting customers and gave them a thankful smile— and maybe he even threw in a little smolder.

But Val was not having any of it and she followed Sam out of the store. "Wow. You really interrupted all those people for your precious Italian leather wallet? That's what was so important you almost knocked me over?"

He stopped, turned to her, and lifted an eyebrow. "Yes? Are you kidding? Of course I did."

"You know—" she put her fists on her hips and narrowed her eyes "—

it's one thing for you to walk around school like you own the whole place. But the *mall?* You're not that important."

He huffed. "Why do you even care? You hate the mall. And the school. And honestly, everything, I think? Do you enjoy anything, Valerie? Tell me what that thing is so I can avoid it forever."

"Ugh, you are *so* infuriating!"

"Right back atcha!"

"Well, how would you like it if I pushed *you* over?"

Valerie stomped up to him, intent on throwing her whole body into him just to show him how annoying it was. But the minute she jammed her shoulder into his torso, everything went black. No—she hadn't passed out. Everyone around them let out a startled little gasp.

Every single light, even the emergency lights, cell phones, *everything* went dark. It was almost like an EMP had hit them out of nowhere, wreaking havoc on the entire mall.

Sam suddenly felt a searing pain in his head, and he reached up to clutch it. His thoughts briefly went to Tony before he fell to his knees, Val at his side.

Tony, at that moment, had taken Ana's arm in an effort to turn her around to get rid of her. But when the lights had gone out, he felt the same headache, and everything left his mind for a few seconds.

When the power came back on, two sets of screams could be heard across the mall. Sam had opened his eyes, only to see his own body kneeling in front of him. And Tony had seen himself, clutching his soaking wet notebook in one hand and Ana's arm in the other. Only, Ana's arm was mysteriously now his own!

# Chapter Two

"What. Did. You. *Do*?" Gasping at how deep her voice had suddenly gotten, Val clutched at her throat. Her doppelganger—presumably the very dashing Samuel Dekker—stood across from her, peering at her through *her* eyes.

"I didn't do anything!" he squeaked as his eyes narrowed. "*You're* the one who was following me around, being a creep, and now..."

Sam's breathing quickened as he looked down at himself. He put his hands on the hem of the oversized brown sweater Val had put on that morning, tugging on it roughly, before wiping his hands down...*her* loose jeans.

Her mouth dropped open as she watched him continue to feel every part of her body. Stepping forward, she said in a low voice, "What are you *doing*?"

"Wondering why you wear such bad clothes," he said in a distracted voice. "Especially when there's such a nice body under here."

Heat flooded her face as she thought about just how *close* he was to her body. And how she was in his! "Samuel Dekker, I swear if you don't give my body back this *instant*—"

"Chill," he said, putting up his hands defensively. There were too many people milling around them. None of them seemed to have been mysteriously catapulted out of their own bodies. And they also didn't seem to be paying any attention to Sam and Val. "I don't want to be in this body any more than I want you to be in mine."

Well, that just made her feel even more indignant. Crossing her arms, she asked, "What's wrong with *me* being in your body?"

His whole face scrunched up—much the same way hers did when other people confused "you're" and "your." "I don't want *anyone* else to be in my body. But yelling at me in a crowded mall isn't going to help anything. Let's just go find Tony."

He turned around and she had no choice but to follow him. It wasn't hard to keep up with him using his own long strides—even in his incredibly tight jeans. Unbelievable as it might have been to him, she wasn't accustomed to wearing such close-fitting clothes.

She grabbed his—or rather, her own—elbow and tugged a little too hard. He skidded to a halt and nearly lost his footing before she caught him. His eyes narrowing, he straightened and pushed her hands away.

"Look, I know you're mad," he said, "but do you really need to drag me around like that?"

"I didn't mean to," she said quickly. "You're just a lot stronger than I thought."

He stared at her for a moment before half his mouth quirked up in a slow smile. "Yeah, I mean, I work out."

"*Sam.*"

"*Okay.*" He patted down his clothes unnecessarily. "Let's find Tony, please. By now he's probably totally lost track of my stuff and I'll be lucky if it hasn't been stolen."

"Your stuff?" she asked as he once again continued toward the centre of the mall.

"Yeah, my clothes I just bought?" He rolled his eyes. "That's why I had to go back to the store. Because I left my—"

"Italian leather wallet—"

"After buying a bunch of clothes, yeah." He lifted an eyebrow. "Why do you sound so annoyed by that?"

"Why do you need a wallet made out of Italian leather?" she asked.

He paused a moment as they manoeuvred around a group of tweens all clumped together in the middle of the hall. "Are you, like, a vegan, or something?"

"Or something," she mumbled.

"Huh?"

"I said—" She stopped and huffed as Sam quickly crossed to the other side of the hall to avoid an older couple who were walking at their own pace. Once she'd caught up to him, she said, "I just like to make sensible purchases. That's all."

"Oh, me, too," he said, sounding like he meant it. "That's why I came today, because there are a bunch of sales on."

"But the wallet—"

"*What* is your deal, Valerie?" he said a little too loudly. A young woman who was handing out flyers by a popcorn kiosk flicked a curious glance at him. Of course, *he* looked like Val, so it probably seemed weird for him to call her Valerie.

Lowering his voice, he said, "Why are you so hung up on my wallet? Don't you think we have something bigger to deal with here?"

Swallowing down her irritation, she had to agree that he was right. She didn't have to agree out loud, but she could at least quietly drop the issue. "Okay, well… What are we going to do about this?"

"I need to find Tony."

"Because he'll…switch us back?"

"No, because he has my stuff. Keep up, Val." Sam snapped his fingers at her. "And also because his sister is supposed to be picking us up in like... Oh, geez. Where's my phone? What time is it?"

Val patted her front pockets, which were mysteriously empty. But the back pockets... Sighing, she reached into both of them with great effort. The fancy wallet came out of the left pocket and Sam's phone was in the right one. "Here..."

He quickly grabbed his phone and shrieked when he saw the time. Maddy, Tony's sister, had probably been waiting for a good ten minutes by now. How was he supposed to explain his tardiness to her and Tony?

"Okay, here's the deal." He gave the phone back. "You need to go home with Tony."

She popped a hip out to put a hand on and gave him a dead stare. "You're kidding, right? You want me to...pretend to be you?"

"Maybe just...just for a little while?" He reached up to scratch his head but when he felt the tight coils of her hair, he dropped his hand. This was weird. "I can't not go home right now. And...and won't your family be worried if you don't go home either?"

Groaning, she put her face in her hands. They would be especially worried and annoyed if they found out she was spending time with a boy like Sam. "Okay," she said quietly. "Okay, let's find Tony."

She started to go again, but he stopped her. "Val... Can I have my phone back?"

She hesitated, her hand reaching out. "People will notice we don't have our own phones. Or...were we going to get some help?"

"I don't know yet," he said quietly. "We can probably figure this out on our own. But I guess—you're right. At least give me your phone number."

Nodding, Val agreed to switch numbers with him. Unlocking his phone was alarmingly easy since all she had to do was stick her finger against the fingerprint scanner. Hers had a code, which she reluctantly gave him. Once they'd saved their own numbers in the other's phone, they both shoved the phones in their pockets and finally continued on their path to find Tony.

*     *     *

The minute Tony and Ana realized they'd switched bodies, they had both recoiled in sheer horror and shock. While the other mall shoppers irritably strode around them, they stood stock still, their eyes wide and mouths hanging open.

"Ana?" Tony breathed as he stared into his own baby blues.

She swallowed hard, her Adam's apple bobbing. "Yeah, it's me," she whispered.

"I'm only going to say this once," he said slowly. "Put my notebook *down*."

Her jaw dropped open, and she stared at him for a moment, trying to decide if he was serious. "You're still worried about *this* thing—" she waved his book, its pages flopping wetly "—when we're like *this*?"

"I haven't finished freaking out about *that* yet. Hand it over."

Ana chewed on her lip—before remembering it was *his* lip—and then said, "Bat for the book."

Rolling his eyes, he held out the bat. She quickly grabbed it with her free hand and practically shoved the moist book at him. "And now?"

"*Oh*." With the book in one hand, he used the other hand to pat down his newly received body. "Oh…oh no. No no. What happened?"

"Can you stop?" Ana hissed under her breath.

She glanced around but it didn't seem like anyone even cared that it looked like Ana was feeling herself up. She grabbed Tony's hand and they both stilled as he gave her an alarmed look. Of course—now it just seemed like Tony was holding hands with her. With a huff, she let go and took a tiny step back.

"Sorry," he mumbled. But he couldn't help running his hand along the long light brown ponytail he was now sporting. "This is weird. How did this happen?"

"Now, how am *I* supposed to know that?" Ana tossed her hands in the air. "You were the one being all jittery and stuff. You probably electrocuted us with your stupid book."

"Okay, first of all—" Tony squeezed the bridge of his delicate nose "—that's not how electrocution works. And second, *you* were the one being an idiot."

Ana reached out and grabbed the front of his shirt to pull him forward. "You take that back," she snipped.

Tony's gaze slid to the confused glances of the few shoppers who had dared to stop and stare at them. Looking back at Ana, he said quietly, "You might want to let me go. You're making me look like a violent man-child."

Startled, Ana looked up and down her own body, which she hadn't meant to be so rough with. She let him go too hard and he stumbled before catching himself. He patted his shirt down, but when he continued patting a little too much and a little too *everywhere*, Ana tapped one of his hands.

"Stop that," she whispered.

"*Sorry.* I'm just trying to figure out…what…happened." He glanced back at the water fountain, grateful the rushing sound was mostly drowning out their conversation. There was no way they'd be able to explain this to anyone else.

"We know what happened," she said. "We need to know how to fix it."

"Okay…okay…" He put a hand up to his head, as if that would help him think harder. But all it did was remind him that he was touching Ana's head, not his own. And her hair was so smooth, he realized as he ran a hand over it again.

"Is that helping you?" she said, almost sounding amused.

Feeling his face flushing, he mumbled, "Not really. Look, we can't stay at the mall forever. Maddy! She's probably waiting for me. You need to go home with her."

Her whole face scrunched up. "You want me to go home with a girl named Maddy?"

"She's my *sister*."

"Oh."

"Yeah. And she's taking me and Sam home. Oh no! He'll be here any minute. Look, just…act normal and we'll figure this out later."

She shook her head, but knew she didn't have much choice. Especially since her own family would be expecting her home soon. And on top of that, she could see Sam out of the corner of her eye… With Valerie Davis?

"Um, does Sam normally hang out with Val or…?"

Ana gestured to where she saw them, and Tony turned with a confused frown. He shook his head, but there was really no more time for discussion as Sam and Val seemed on a mission to get to them as quickly as possible. But of course, they had no idea that Sam and Val weren't exactly themselves.

Stopping in front of them, Val turned to Ana and said, "Hello, Anthony."

"Samuel," Ana said. "Hi."

"It's time to go," Val said.

Ana nodded. "Yes, it is."

The boys looked at the girls who were in their bodies, giving them the most disgusted looks for not properly portraying them. Then Sam's gaze dropped to the book in Tony's hands.

"*Um*—" He came closer and touched the booked gingerly. "Why is this book so wet?"

"I dropped it in the fountain!" Tony said quickly.

"No, *I* dropped it," Ana corrected. "Because I'm very clumsy."

"You're not *that* clumsy," Sam said.

Ana turned to him, staring down at him with her eyebrows lowered over her eyes. "What do you even care, ice queen? Like, how would you even know? It's not like you hang out with him—*me*."

"I—" Val opened and closed her mouth. Why did everyone call her that?

Tony glared at Ana. "I was being an idiot and swinging my bat around." He raised the bat and jiggled it a bit. "And I made, er, him drop the book."

Ana just rolled her eyes. But Sam stepped towards her and said, "Well, you should probably take that home and dry it so nothing worse happens to it."

"And you should probably give that bat to someone who knows what they're doing with it," Val said, nodding at the bat in Ana's hands.

Tony and Ana looked at each other. They were loathe to do it but if they didn't, Val and Sam would be even more suspicious than they already were. So they very slowly exchanged the items, trying not to make it look like this was the worst day of their lives.

"Okay, bye," Ana said, turning quickly.

"Bye," Tony whispered.

"Wait for me," Sam said. Ana and Tony frowned at him, and he had to consciously stop himself from smacking his forehead. "I mean wait for Sam. *Sam*, didn't you say you had a bunch of stuff to take home?"

"Your stuff is still on the bench," Tony said. "It's safe."

"Oh…" Val looked over at the mass of bags. Why did Sam need all that stuff? This was ridiculous. But…she still picked them all up and reluctantly followed Ana who had started walking away again.

The boys stood there, watching their own retreating bodies, not knowing how they were supposed to get through this—especially without each other's help.

# Chapter Three

Val and Ana walked woodenly to the exit of the mall, neither of them knowing quite what to do with themselves. And without the knowledge that the other "boy" wasn't quite himself either, they didn't even notice how weird they were both acting.

Val's arms ached with all the bags she had to carry. And Ana's hands ached to have her bat back and get rid of this sopping mess of a book.

When they reached the doors of the mall, Ana stopped abruptly. Tony's sister was supposed to be waiting for them, but she had no idea what Maddy looked like.

"What's wrong?" Val asked, sounding far more irritated than she'd meant to.

"Nothing," Ana said quickly. "I'm just looking for...my sister."

"Do you see her?"

"No. Do you?"

Val's face scrunched up. "Why would I ask you that if I'd seen her?"

"Okay, *sorry.*"

"What does she even look like?" popped out of Val's mouth before she could stop herself.

As if that weren't bad enough, Ana's first and erroneous reaction was, "I don't know!"

Val turned to her, lifting one eyebrow, and wondering what could possibly be wrong with *Tony*. "You…you don't know what your own sister looks like?"

Ana could feel her face flushing, and with Tony's pale colouring, it was probably super obvious. "What I meant was—"

"*Tony*" came an annoyed but also somewhat relieved female voice from behind them. "Sam. There you are. I've been waiting forever. I can't believe I had to get out of the car to find you two."

Val and Ana turned around to find a gorgeous girl with wavy blond hair, blue eyes, and a scowl on her face. Maddy, presumably.

"That's what she looks like," Ana said.

"Of course it is," Val said, trying to sound like Sam.

Tilting her head, Maddy put a hand on her hip and narrowed her eyes. "Are you guys seriously making fun of me? After I dropped you off here *and* came back for you? Come on. Ty's making some elaborate meal and if we don't eat it while it's hot, he'll be annoyed."

Val had no desire to share a meal with anyone but her own family. Even then, that was iffy some days, since they were never quiet long enough to give her a moment to think. But that was still preferable to pretending to be Sam! She trailed behind the other two, wondering how she was supposed to survive long enough to get back together with Sam so she could get her body back.

Ana, who had no idea of the thoughts whirling inside Val's head, was also internally freaking out. She'd already managed to upset Tony's sister. It wouldn't be long before Maddy could tell something was off about her little brother. Ana didn't even know Tony well enough to pretend to be him. This was a huge mistake. They should have stayed at the mall a while longer, maybe even long enough for another blackout.

But now she was stuck trying to pretend to be best friends with Sam, arguably the second most pretentious boy at their school. Tony took the top spot, of course. Always walking around with books in his head and ink stains on his hands from writing all the time. Like he was *so* much more intellectual than the rest of them.

Val would have agreed with Ana on both counts. If, of course, Val knew that Ana was in the same car thinking them. As it was, she was squirming around in her seat, trying to fathom how Sam could ever be comfortable in these clothes. Nothing seemed to sit quite right, and Val didn't even want to think about why or how to fix it. She just wanted her own body and clothes back.

"So, what'd you end up getting?" Maddy asked out of the blue. When no one answered her, Maddy prompted, "Sam? What'd you get at the mall."

"Oh, *me*," Val said quickly. "Umm. Uh. I got, um…" She looked in the bags quickly and ran her hands over the expensive-looking fabrics. Boy, Sam sure was something else, wasn't he? "I got some clothes."

"Yeah, but—" Maddy stopped and chuckled. "Okay, I can wait till we're at the apartment to see them. That does make more sense."

"Mmhmm…"

Val looked out the window and watched the houses passing. They'd already gone straight past her neighbourhood. She lived within walking distance of the mall. Which Sam didn't even know! She quickly reached for his phone and, with incredibly difficulty, pulled it out of its tight but deep pocket.

**Val: 24 Lovers Lane**

**Sam: What about it?**

Val sighed aloud. *How* could he be so pretty but so stupid?

## Val: That's my ADDRESS

Sam never answered back, which just made her fret more. She wanted to ask more questions, but Maddy had slowed down and was turning into a bumpy parking lot. She parked in one of the empty spaces, turned the car off, and then got out. Val and Ana stayed in their seats though, neither of them knowing quite what to do with themselves.

Maddy tapped on Ana's window, since she was sitting in the seat behind the driver's side. When Maddy frowned at her, Ana realized it would have been far more natural for her—Maddy's "brother"—to get out and follow.

Ana reluctantly unbuckled while Val tried to gather up all the infernal bags. When Ana got out, she nearly left the book behind, but Maddy pointed it out. It was only then that Maddy noticed the damage done to it.

"*Tony*," she said in an incredulous voice. "Your book! What happened?"

"It fell in the fountain," Ana said flatly.

"Oh no!" Maddy put a hand up to her forehead as she cringed at the book. "No wonder you were so quiet on the drive. Bring it in, quick. We can fix this."

"Okay..." What was it about this book that everyone was *so* worried over it? Ana kind of had bigger issues to deal with right now! Of course, Maddy didn't know that. And if Ana said it, no one would believe her.

Maddy rushed into the building and towards the stairwell while Ana trailed behind her, and Val struggled to not lose any of the bags out in the parking lot. Neither girl wanted to get lost in an unfamiliar building, but they also didn't want to be there at all. Nothing about this felt right.

They followed Maddy up to the third floor, where she went to an apartment in the middle of the long hall. The girls in boy's bodies both tried to come in behind her at the same time. Ana, being Ana, fully knocked Val over in the hallway, and Val, being Val, dropped the bags. Scowling at Ana, Val was tempted to leave all that stuff since she didn't even care about it. But guilt got the best of her, and she leaned over to grab it.

With Val out of the way, Ana came into the apartment just in time to hear a male voice call out, "Hey, what took you guys so long?"

"Tony dropped his book in the fountain!" Maddy said frantically.

Ana looked around as a delicious smell reached her nose. The place was pretty tidy and neat, but kind of plain. They had walked into an open living room/dining room combo. The living room had a brown three-seater couch and a mismatched black recliner in front of a TV with a black box and two gaming systems. The large bay window had blinds and no curtains.

The dining room set had six chairs, two of which didn't match. There was no tablecloth on the table, but there was plenty of other...stuff. Some tools, a couple of textbooks, a stack of opened envelopes, a used cup on a coaster, and what looked like half a diorama someone was working on.

The kitchen was beyond a half wall that separated it from the dining room. There were three other rooms off to the sides, hidden behind closed doors. Ana assumed those were the bathroom and bedrooms. On the wall between the kitchen and the first door was a large framed picture of Sam wearing some bougie dress shirt that was half undone and pouting into the camera's lens.

Ana didn't even get a chance to roll her eyes before an older, more broad-shouldered version of Sam stepped out of the kitchen, his hands clad in oven mitts. "Are you serious? Do you want to put it in rice?"

"It's not a phone, Ty," Maddy said in exasperation. "We can just dry it with Sam's hairdryer. You don't mind, do you, Sam? Sam?"

Ana looked back to the door where Val was finally coming in, half of Sam's acquisitions out of the bags and laying haphazardly in her arms. She immediately went over to the couch and dumped everything on it. She sighed in relief and turned to the others, who were all staring at her curiously. That was when she saw the large photo of Sam, which she frowned at.

"Sam," Maddy said after a weighted moment. "I'm going to use your hairdryer on Tony's book, okay?"

"Yeah, fine, whatever," Val said tersely.

What did she care if they used Sam's hairdryer? She was so accustomed to everyone at home helping themselves to whatever. Hardly anything she owned was wholly reserved for her alone. And besides, the hairdryer *wasn't* hers. She reached up and touched the hair currently on her head. He didn't even have enough hair to warrant needing to dry it with a hairdryer.

"Sam."

*Ugh*, Val was already tired of hearing that name. This time it was said by, she assumed, his older brother. "Yes?"

"Clear the table, would you?"

He went back into the kitchen, cutting off any potential arguments. Val didn't necessarily mind setting the table for dinner. But when the table looked like *that* and she had no idea where any of it went, it made her want to turn and run. Maybe Tony could help out.

"Tony," Val said. Ana didn't move an inch and was busy staring at the picture of Sam. "*Tony*."

"Huh?" This time, Ana turned towards Val, her eyes wide. "Oh, yeah, me. What's up?"

Val gestured to the table. "Do you want to help me?"

"Not really." Val frowned in confusion and Ana laughed. "But you're my best friend," Ana said quickly. "So obviously I'll help."

They went to the table and each of them picked up various items, looking at each one before setting it back down. Ana was waiting for Val to take the lead on where to put everything, not knowing that Val was hoping Ana would know where everything went. Finally, they mutually agreed on putting everything—even the tools—on the part of the couch that wasn't covered in clothes.

They had the table cleared off and a tablecloth placed on it by the time Ty was coming out of the kitchen with a large pan of homemade lasagna. He smiled at the tablecloth, but then his gaze slid to the couch.

"You boys are cleaning that up after dinner, right?" Ty said dryly.

"Of course," Ana said flicking her wrist. "We would never leave a couch looking like that. That's for crazy people." Like her family, who found a way to make every available surface a storage area.

"Yeah, not in *my* apartment," Ty said, narrowing his eyes the slightest bit. "I don't care if I'm dating your sister, I'll ban you if you trash the place."

"Ohhhh, you're *dating* her," Ana said. "That makes so much sense."

Ty blinked at Ana and then turned to Val with an eyebrow lifted. "Is he okay? Or is he all messed up because of his book?"

"I have no idea," Val said honestly. She couldn't tell if this was normal behaviour for Tony because she tried everything possible to limit her interactions with both Tony and Sam.

Ty looked back and forth between both of them, looking like he was trying to do complicated math in his head. "Okay… I can see you're both very hungry. Let's…let's eat."

"That's probably a good idea," Ana said, realizing now that some of the nervousness in her stomach was actually just hunger pangs.

Val nodded, and sat in the nearest chair. But by the look on Ty's face, she'd chosen wrong. She rose and went around to each of the other chairs until Ty's expression returned to normal. *This* one was Sam's chair. The one that very specifically faced his big picture. Great.

# Chapter Four

Tony held Ana's bat loosely, wishing he hadn't just watched Ana walk off with his book. He just desperately hoped Sam would help her dry it off.

The only problem was that...Sam was right next to him. In Val's body. And Tony had no way of knowing that. Sam was staring in the general direction Val had taken his body, wondering if he'd made the biggest mistake of his life.

"Hey," Tony said, immediately gaining Sam's attention. "Take a picture, it'll last longer."

"What?" Sam asked, his eyebrows drawn in.

"Sam. Take his picture." Tony frowned. "I didn't know you were into him, but he's pretty picky so, like, good luck with that."

Sam let out a sound that was somewhere between a scoff and a laugh. *He* was picky? That was news to him. "What do you even know, Ana? Have you even had, like, one conversation with him?"

Tony's face went red. Of course, Sam thought he was Ana, and now it probably looked like Ana was making snarky, jealous statements. "No, it's just... No. Sorry. Forget I said anything, Val."

Sam rolled his eyes. Now it looked like Val was into Sam and defending him and that was just too messed up. "I have to go," Sam said, wanting to get away from Ana. If he'd known Ana was Tony, Sam never would have left his side.

Instead, he stomped away. Val had given him her address and he guessed he was just supposed to go there. And pretend he was her and act like everything was okay. But to what end? He couldn't pretend to be Val forever.

24 Lovers Lane was a five-minute walk from the mall, Sam noticed with only a short amount of jealousy. It was the smallest house on a street where no two houses were alike. Some of them were huge, likely 5-bedroom homes. Some, like Val's, were more modest. Hers looked like a backsplit, and it was on a corner lot, too. Did Val know how lucky she was to have such a nice yard? If Sam had a yard like this, he would definitely get a—

A deep bark cut off his line of thinking. A huge dog came running straight towards him, a German shepherd by the looks of it. Smiling, Sam reached out his hand to it. It sniffed him, barked a couple of times, and then barked again.

"Shh," Sam said as the dog kept barking. He scratched behind its ears and patted its back. Although it was super friendly, it seemed a little put off by Sam's presence. "It's just me. *Val.*"

The dog barked even louder, prompting someone to open the front door and shout at Sam. Or…they were shouting at Val, but Val wasn't there to respond to them.

"Val, what is going on?"

Sam looked up at the middle-aged woman with dark, straightened hair, a pencil skirt, and a crisp white blouse. The woman—Mrs. Davis, Sam assumed— had a hand on her hip and was scowling at him. Sam put his hands up in surrender and slowly made his way towards the door. The dog followed him, nudging his hands and nearly tripping him by sidling up against him.

"Come, come," Mrs. Davis said, flailing her hand. Her frown deepened. "What took you so long at the mall?"

"You wouldn't believe me if I told you," he accidentally blurted out as he took himself up the porch stairs.

"Try me."

Sam looked up at her in surprise. She sounded so much like Ty the one time Sam had snuck out of the apartment late at night. The reason he'd snuck out was silly—Tony had wanted to do some "research" on the night sky, but it had to be at 3:23 a.m. exactly and Sam would never not do something Tony wanted to do. But he didn't think Ty would take that explanation and his response had been the same as Mrs. Davis's: "Try me."

Sam snorted and that just made her eyebrows draw in even more. "Sorry," he said quickly. "I shouldn't have been so late."

"No, you shouldn't have been. Go help Juliette."

Nodding, Sam stepped through the doorway. There were a several pairs of shoes lined up on a shoe rack next to the door, so he stepped out of Val's sensible closed-toed shoes before going farther in. He'd never been to Val's house before, but all houses were basically the same. Stairs by the front entrance led to another floor. A hallway with two doors in it—likely the bathroom and basement stairs— led to what he assumed was the kitchen. To his right, a pristine living room.

Unidentifiable spices wafted towards him, and his stomach gurgled. He made his way down the hall, his eye catching briefly on a family photo that featured Val, her parents, and a younger boy and girl. The girl must have been Juliette, her sister.

He peeked his head into the kitchen where Juliette was stirring something in a Dutch oven. Whatever it was smelled delicious, and his stomach groaned again. Juliette turned around, giggling, and then pointed her wooden spoon at him.

"You were supposed to help me with dinner tonight," she complained playfully.

He shrugged. It looked like she had everything under control, but he came closer anyway. "What...can I do?"

"See if the biscuits are ready." Juliette once again gestured with her spoon, this time at the oven.

Glancing around the kitchen, he found a pair of floral oven mitts, put them on, and then opened the oven. It groaned as he hefted the door down and then let out a puff of steam straight into his face. The biscuits looked…flaky and golden and perfect enough to make Sam salivate. He pulled the tray out.

"Can you make the gravy?"

"Make the…?"

Sam set the tray of biscuits down and looked around for anything that even remotely resembled gravy mix. Oh—Juliette was handing him a pan with some random broth in it. Sam could cook as much as his brother had taught him. They were fairly self-sufficient. But nothing they made was complicated. He certainly didn't know how to make gravy from scratch.

"Maybe I should set the table instead," Sam said, knowing he could easily accomplish that.

Juliette glanced at him, one sassy eyebrow raised. "That's Harrison's job tonight. Since you didn't help with dinner, the least you could do is make the gravy."

Sam put his arms around himself, realized he was basically just holding Val's body, and let them drop abruptly. "Okay…"

While Juliette busied herself getting the dinner she'd made onto serving dishes, Sam pulled out his phone to look up how to make gravy. Thankfully it seemed simple enough. Just mix some flour and water in it? He could do that.

Or…he thought he could do that. He put some flour in the broth and stirred it, but it didn't look right. Referring back to the instructions online, he realized his error. Ah, he had to heat it. Easy peasy. Sort of. It still didn't seem right, and he was probably missing more steps, but the family was starting to gather at the table and the gravy was bubbling.

He turned the stove off and looked for a separate dish to put it in. That should have been easy. Most people had a plain old white gravy bowl. But Sam didn't find anything like that. With a sigh, Juliette came over to him and reached into a cupboard past his head. She pulled out the most elaborate gravy dish Sam had ever seen. Porcelain—he guessed—with a blue floral design that ran throughout it, a handle that looked like it would break if he held it wrong, and a spout that seemed to go on forever.

Juliette dumped his gravy into it, her eyes narrowing more with every clump that fell into it. But she didn't say anything. She just brought the gravy over to the table and waited for Sam. He went over to the one empty seat left at the table, the one next to Harrison. No one had food yet and as soon as Sam sat, they all bowed their heads.

Oh. He could handle one prayer. Except…no one prayed. They just all stayed silent for a moment before Mr. Davis announced emphatically, "Amen."

After that, they passed around the food in a frenzy. There was a roast that practically fell apart, golden roasted potatoes, sautéed green beans, biscuits, and…Sam's lumpy gravy. His mouth watered and he hastily grabbed as much as possible. Mrs. Davis gave him a side glance, and Mr. Davis lifted a quiet eyebrow.

But it was Harrison who said, "Valerie, wow, slow down. We need to eat, too."

The rest of the family chuckled at the joke, but Sam felt awkward and embarrassed. The way he'd filled his plate was no different than he would have done it at home. But he also had to admit that at home, when it was just him and Ty, they didn't really care much for decorum. So he slowed down a bit and then took a bite of the roast. It was even better than he imagined.

He looked up and found Juliette staring at him. "What?"

"This gravy is super lumpy."

He nodded. It was. He knew it was and that was why he hadn't taken any. "I'm sorry I ruined your biscuits," he said quietly.

"It's fine." Juliette waved her hand dismissively. "Just…don't ever again."

Sam had no intention of ever having to help Juliette make dinner again. But how was he supposed to avoid that if he didn't know how to get back into his own body?

*      *      *

Tony had taken Ana's bat—and her body—and left the mall in a quiet panic. When they'd agreed to just chill like this for a few hours, it had seemed like a good idea. But now that Tony was approaching Ana's house, his body was giving him all kinds of warning signs. His back was aching, he felt nauseous, and he was one loud sound away from a full-blown migraine.

Oh... Ana was on her period. Well, that explained *that*. But why did it have to hurt so much?

Tony vowed to raid the medicine cabinet as soon as he got to the address Ana had texted him. But when he got there, he stopped short on the sidewalk. Sparse grass grew across the yard and in between the cracks of the pathway that led to the porch. Ahead, past the two columns with peeling paint that supported a portico, was a storm door with a ripped screen. To the left of the front door was a wide window that was so dirty Tony didn't think he'd be able to spy through it. To the right, a set of sagging lawn chairs and a dish filled with cigarette butts on a glass-top table between them.

He'd never felt more uncomfortable in his life, and that had little to do with being in Ana's body. It was her home—if he could even call it that—that made him feel terribly out of place. Having no other choice, however, he went up to the door and found it unlocked. There were no cars in the driveway, but someone had to be home, right?

"Hello?" Tony called out tentatively, surprising himself by hearing Ana's voice come out of his body. Who else's voice would it be, though?"

"Ana?" a frail voice called back. "*Rápido, rápido...*"

Great. Tony's Spanish was terrible. He followed the woman's voice through the house, which admittedly wasn't as bad inside as outside. Sure, the wallpaper was an outdated stripey pattern, and the parquet flooring was scuffed from everyday use. There also seemed to be stuff on every flat surface. Tons of shoes crowded on the mat by the door, backpacks and bags on the floor of the hallway, a little pile of receipts, pens, candy wrappers, and other refuse on a table. But it was…kind of homey. Especially with pictures of Ana's family hung on the wall.

And when he saw the living room with its mismatched couches, too many blankets and pillows, and an old lady in a recliner with a patchwork quilt overtop of her, it felt even more cozy. Then the woman started speaking rapid-fire Spanish at him and he was frozen in his spot.

"Oh, um, hi…*abuela?*" he said.

The woman scoffed, waved her hand, and started her explanation all over again. In the middle of it, she burst out laughing and then patted the arm of the couch next to her. Tony, not having a clue what to do, sat on the couch. He still had Ana's bat clutched awkwardly in his hand and now he wondered what he was supposed to do with her grandmother.

Abuela pulled a remote control from somewhere among her blanket and pointed it at the TV. She flicked the channel a few times until it landed on—of all things—a Blue Jays game. Just what Tony needed. To watch baseball with Señora Dellagusta.

Tony tried to pretend to watch the game so as not to offend the older lady while he secretly took out his phone. Or rather, he took out Ana's phone and texted…himself? Her? Them? Ugh.

**Tony: I don't speak Spanish and I don't understand a thing your abuela's saying…**

**Ana: It doesn't matter. She has Alzheimer's and I can't understand her most of the time either.**

**Tony: That's not very helpful.**

**Ana: Well, neither is having dinner with your sister and her boyfriend and Sam, but here we are.**

**Tony: Let's meet tonight.**

**Ana: Yes. I want my bat back.**

**Tony: And your body?**

**Ana: That was a given.**

Tony rolled his eyes. Of course, Ana wanted her bat *and* her body. He assumed she meant he had better bring the bat tonight, otherwise he was in even more trouble.

# Chapter Five

Ana chewed on her lip, impatiently waiting for this weird family dinner to end already. Maddy had complimented Ty's cooking ten times and yeah, it was nice enough, but it wasn't all that. And neither was he! He hardly ever smiled, though he did compliment Maddy back a few times. Oh, what Ana wouldn't give to be with Abuela.

How could she have forgotten about Abuela's Alzheimer's and her recent inability to speak English? She *could* speak it. She'd spoken it most of Ana's life, though they went back and forth between English and Spanish often enough. But since the diagnosis last year, Abuela had slowly reverted back to Spanish only.

Ana looked at the boy she thought was Sam, but he was far more silent than she was used to. At school, Sam was one of the popular kids, if only because he was so extroverted and fun. Not *her* kind of fun, but fun to a lot of people. But now he sat sullen, his lips locked up tight. Ana didn't know that behind those dark eyes was Valerie.

Valerie, who wouldn't have made lumpy gravy, who would have made half of Juliette's dinner without complaint, who would have taken the dog out. Valerie was struggling just as much as Ana was, though there was no way either girl could have known that.

"Um." Ana cleared her throat. "I kind of have to go home. I have…stuff. To do."

"I also have…things," Valerie added.

"Oh, yeah, and your book!" Maddy rose quickly, taking her plate and Ty's.

"Don't worry," Ty said, taking the dishes from her with a small smile. "We'll clean up. It's fine."

"Thanks, babe."

She leaned down to give him a kiss that felt a little too long. Ana looked at Sam—*Val*, and they both rolled their eyes and looked away uncomfortably.

"Okay, bye, Sam," Ana said loudly when it had been a good ten seconds.

"Bye, Tony." Val rose from her chair, and the scraping sound finally caused the happy couple to break apart.

Maddy got the book from where it had been left to dry and handed it gently to Ana. Ana didn't particularly want to handle it, but she felt bad she'd played a very small part in it getting wet. Plus, she felt sure Tony would never return her bat without this book in exchange.

Ana rushed out of the apartment while Maddy gave Ty one more "short" kiss.

As they left, Maddy teasingly said, "I know. You think it's gross that I'm dating your best friend's brother."

Ana thought a lot of things. She thought it was weird Sam only lived with his brother, and that someone like Maddy would go for someone like Ty, and also that being in a boy's body was horrible and she wanted out of it.

But instead of all that, she muttered, "Just the kissing."

Maddy laughed airily. "I've seen you do some pretty gross kissing, Tony. Give me a break."

Ana lifted an eyebrow. What kind of girls would Tony kiss like *that*? She was tempted to ask, but didn't. And she hoped she wouldn't be forced to kiss any of them. She had better things to do with her time. Like getting back in her body and playing her game on Saturday.

On the way Ana kept texting Tony, only to get non-answers from him. She wanted to know how Abuela was, but how could he know when he couldn't understand her? She asked if anyone else had come home and noticed she wasn't...exactly herself. His answer was to ask if anyone had noticed *he* was being weird.

"Oh, Stella's here," Maddy said as she pulled into the driveway of a nice two-story home. "What a nice surprise for us."

Ana, being a girl, could hear the complex notes of insecurity, longing, and irritation in Maddy's voice. She and Stella were obviously on good terms, but she could tell Stella wasn't her best friend. And when she saw Stella for herself, she knew undoubtedly this had to be another sister of Tony's. Hopefully he didn't have anymore hiding in the shadows.

Stella and Maddy air-kissed each others' cheeks and greeted each other in a sickly sweet way. Stella loosely grasped Maddy's shoulders and Maddy had her hands on Stella's elbows. Stella and Maddy stepped through the front door together and Ana trailed behind them.

"Are you ready to see the first photos from my photoshoot?" Stella asked, her eyes twinkling.

"Of course," Maddy said, matching her energy.

Stella turned to Ana and smiled nicely at her. "You, too? Oh, where's Sam? He would probably be interested, too!"

Ana just shrugged, wondering why Sam would care about seeing photos from Stella's photoshoot. Oh, no, were they...salacious? Was Sam into Tony's eldest sister? Gross.

"If I'd known you were coming over tonight I would have asked him,"

Maddy said with exaggerated patience. "But that's fine. He'll figure out the whole process on his own soon, anyway. Right, Tony?"

"Uh huh," Ana mumbled. What were they going on about? Ana excused herself before Stella could even think to open the thick envelope with fancy writing that was sitting on the front hall table. She cared very little about Stella's pictures and very much about getting her body back.

She was halfway up the stairs before Tony's sisters called her—or rather *him*—again. But she brushed them off, saying she had a lot of homework to do. Really, she just wanted to track down Tony and her body and get her body back and never look Tony in the eye again.

Not wanting to wait any longer or take any more chances, she peeked into the bedrooms upstairs until she found the one that looked most like Tony's and scooted into it. After shutting the door softly, she pulled out her phone to call him.

"Hey," he answered breathlessly.

"Hi." The sound of a baseball cracking against a bat in the background rang through her ear. "You're…still watching with Abuela?"

"I'm not sure what else I'm supposed to do."

"Well, let's…let's meet up. We gotta figure this out." When he hesitated too long, she said, "Tony? Did you hear me?"

"Yeah, yeah. It's just—" He stopped when the crowd roared. "Oh, wow. It's the bottom of the ninth and they're tied. So…"

"Seriously?" But she got it. She wouldn't want to leave a game like that either. "Oh, alright. Meet me at the mall after it's over though."

"Mall's closing soon."

She huffed at the absolute nonchalance in his voice. "I *know*. But that was the scene of the crime, and we should go back there."

"I think it was more of an accident or a fluke than a crime."

"*Tony.*"

"Okay, okay— Oh!" More cheering came in the background. "There it is. The Jays won. Yay, I guess? Do you cheer for them?"

"Obviously." She rolled her eyes. Normally she could go on and on about baseball, but not in her present condition. "Let's meet up now."

"Fine, I'll see you soon."

Ana hung up without saying goodbye and then looked around. She'd pegged this room as Tony's because of the blue comforter on the bed, the white and black striped carpet, and the one green polo shirt that had been left on the back of the chair at the desk. The room was pristine, except for the desk itself, which was covered in papers, sticky notes, two empty water cups, and several writing utensils. There was also a small collection of notebooks lined up nicely at the back along the wall.

Not able to contain her curiosity, Ana came forward and glanced down at the chicken scratch on the most accessible piece of paper. "'Valentino's sword is magic, but where does the magic come from...' What? Who's Valentino?"

Tony's book was still in her hand, and she was tempted to open it, too, but decided against it. She wasn't curious enough to anger Tony if she damaged it any further. She left his room and snuck out before his sisters could see her again. She did *not* want to get sucked into their conversation.

Quickly, she made her way to the mall. Ana was a runner. She had been on running teams before trying baseball. They liked her because she was fast and had only needed a little coaching before pitching. Tony, however, was not a runner, and after only a couple of minutes, his legs were burning. Ana stopped to take in deep breaths, wondering if something was wrong with his lungs or if he just needed to go to the gym once in a while.

This was the worst, but she finally made it to the mall without totally feeling like keeling over. The parking lot was empty save for a few squatters, and she had no idea where Tony would be waiting for her.

"Tony?" Ana called out in a low voice. When there was no answer, she said louder, "Tony!"

"I'm here" came her own voice back to her. "Shh, keep your voice down."

"Well, if you'd answered the first time…" She turned in a circle until she saw him sitting on a bench outside the large bookstore entrance, holding her bat across his knees. He was also mysteriously in a different outfit than she'd put on that morning. "You changed."

"Yeah, I did." He rose and came the few steps down to meet her, loosely dragging the bat behind him. "I sort of…got blood on your other pants, and then figured I might as well change the shirt, too. Sorry."

"Oh. I forgot about that."

His eyebrows drawing in, he looked down. "How does one forget about that?"

Instead of answering him, Ana huffed and closed the gap between them. She reached out to take her bat and said, "Here's your book. It's about as dry as we could get it."

He grabbed the book she shoved at him, dismayed to find it was still damp. "There's nothing dry about this."

"Yeah, well…" Taking her bat several feet away, she started swinging it like she was really hitting a ball out there. She made him look like a real baseball player, which was a weird experience for him.

"Ana, this is serious."

"It's just a notebook, Mr. T."

His scowl deepened and he moved to stand directly in her path. Surely she wouldn't hit her own body with a bat? "It's *not* just a notebook. And also, I was referring to *this*." He gestured back and forth between them.

"Oh, yeah." Ana looked down at Tony's shoes and jeans. His T-shirt with a nerdy pun on it. "I don't like this, T. I want my body back."

"I didn't choose this." He looked down at his own borrowed body, too.

36

Then slowly, they both looked back up at each other. "Your entire body hurts."

Her face softened into an almost sympathetic frown. "Nah... Nah, you're fine. You just gotta stretch."

"Stretch." Licking his lips, he nodded. "I don't think that'll fix anything. But...okay. And then what?"

"Usually, if I just lie down for a bit—"

"Ana, I meant our bodies. What are we supposed to do?"

"Maybe..." She shrugged. "Lie down for a bit and sleep it off?"

He gaped at her. "That's the best you've got?"

Throwing her hands up, she nearly smacked him in the face with her bat. "What do *you* suggest?"

"Well...if this were a book... Hmm." He stroked his chin—or rather, Ana's delicately pointed chin. "We would fall into some sort of portal where a magician or wizard or sorcerer would explain to us *how* we got into this predicament, and using contextual clues based on that, we would figure how to get *out* of said predicament."

"Tony." She shook her head so vehemently he was worried it would fall off. Then she started to laugh. "Tony, Tony, Tony... This isn't a *book*. This is *real life*."

"I know!" He tossed up his hands too, being careful not to let go of his book. "But since this kind of stuff doesn't happen in real life, we'll have to look elsewhere for solutions."

"Okay, why do you talk like that?"

"Like what?"

"Like...like uppity."

Slowly, he lowered his hands as her words sunk in. "Are you seriously upset at my level of vocabulary right now?"

Her eyes narrowed. "Sort of?"

"Listen, *chiquita*—"

"Don't *chiquita* me, white boy."

He rolled his eyes. "Now is not the time for us to be picking petty arguments with each other. Can we just…can we just agree on something? Anything?"

Chewing her lip again, Ana's eyes softened as she thought about it. *Could* they agree on something? Possibly. Sighing, she held her own bat out towards him. "Try to be me for the next day and maybe…maybe this will resolve on its own."

With no small amount of hesitation, Tony came closer. But he didn't take the bat. He knew if he did, he'd have to give something in return. He held his book out and said, "If we do this, do you think you can find a safe spot for my book where it won't get damaged any further, or spied on?"

She nodded gravely. They reached out for the borrowed objects at the same time, hoping beyond hope that something might zap them. But nothing did. They were still stuck in the wrong bodies.

"Ana?"

"Yes."

"You have to try to be nice to Sam, too. He's my best friend in the whole world. If you stick close to him, you'll be fine."

"Alright." She nodded again. "But I can't guarantee I can be that nice to your sisters, too. I don't get their relationship *at all* and I want no part in it."

Tony flicked his wrist. "Ah, forget about them. Just don't let anything happen with Sam."

"Yeah, I'll keep the bromance alive," she promised with a sassy smile. "But you have to go to my baseball practice tomorrow."

Glancing down at the bat in his hand, he said, "Do you really want people to think you're terrible at baseball or…should I call off because your body feels like its eating itself from the inside out?"

"Oh. Yeah. Maybe that second one, then."

Tony nodded. "See you tomorrow at school?"

He held out his hand and Ana put hers in it. Nothing happened and for a second, they just stood there. Then she shook his hand. "Tomorrow."

# Chapter Six

As soon as Maddy and Ana—who Val thought was Tony—had left, Val looked around awkwardly at Sam and Ty's place. Ty finished stacking up the dishes in front of himself and then gestured to them, giving Val a familiar look. She got it—he cooked, she got to clean. It was the same rules in her own home.

*Oh, no!* She was supposed to make dinner with Juliette tonight. Had Sam helped her? Could he even cook? Ty certainly could, but that didn't mean Sam could. Oh, she hoped her sister wasn't too upset over that. Juliette had a tendency to get uptight over the smallest things. Surely Sam could handle that, right?

No. She shook her head. Whether he could or not, she had to get to Sam and get her body back. But…the dishes were staring her in the face. And Ty was walking away. She couldn't just leave them, could she? For Sam's sake—though she felt she owed him nothing—she would load up the dishwasher.

And then she discovered there was no dishwasher. It was her. *She* was the dishwasher.

With a sigh, she rolled her sleeves up to her elbows, tried to ignore Sam's muscular forearms, and filled up the sink with hot water. She knew dishwashers were a privilege, but she had kind of assumed it was one that everyone had by now. She would never complain about their old dishwasher again. Especially when she got to the pots and pans Ty had used. He was a messy cook.

And she couldn't very well leave the kitchen a mess either! She wiped down the counter and stovetop, swept the floor, and even cleaned the coffeemaker. It was when she had the thought to clean out the fridge that she stopped herself. What was she doing? She needed her body back.

Deciding to call Sam and see if they could meet up, she put away her cleaning supplies and left the kitchen. But Ty was sitting in the living room with a textbook and a notebook. No way could she have that conversation out here.

She went to the hallway that was beyond the dining room area and spied the three doors. Two bedrooms and a bathroom, she guessed. Sam's should have been easy enough to find. The first door she opened had a football helmet on top of a pile of other football gear, and unless Sam had recently joined the school team, this wasn't his room.

Val tentatively pushed the other door open. She felt bad invading Sam's privacy like this—but then again, there wasn't much privacy left when bodies had been swapped. She closed the door and then looked for a place to sit. Sam's room wasn't super messy, but the bed was unmade, there were a few pieces of clothing out—lying next to a laundry hamper—and the small desk in the corner was covered in papers.

Curiosity got the better of her and she came closer to inspect the papers. Her eyebrows drew in at the of drawings laid out on the desk. *Good* drawings, too, if she were into fantasy art. There was a pile of sketches on the right-hand side that seemed to correspond to the large full colour one on top. It featured a human-like man with two curly horns on his head and a greenish tinge to his skin. There was a smug grin on his face, partially obscured by two small fangs protruding from his lower jaw. He was riding a majestic black horse with a glorious mane and red eyes.

Val's breath caught in her throat with every detail her eyes found. The glint of the sword the character held. Each individual pencil stroke that made up the hairs of his eyebrows. The swirling black, purple, and blue clouds in the background. Was this really Sam's art? The "SD" in the bottom right-hand corner seemed to indicate so, but Val still had second thoughts.

A buzzing sound pulled her out of her reverie, and she got Sam's phone out of her pocket. Sam! "Hey, how is everything?" she asked urgently.

"Well, other than the lumpy gravy—"

"Who made lumpy gravy?"

"*You* did," he answered, almost sounding like he wanted to laugh.

She rolled her eyes. Poor Juliette. "Oh. Look, let's meet up somewhere and…"

"Force our bodies back to normal?"

"Yeah."

"The school's halfway between us, right? Let's meet there."

"That's fine."

Val sighed as she hung up and glanced once more at horn guy. She couldn't linger on this. She had a body to get back.

When she went out to the living room, she found Ty still on the couch and said, "Is it okay if I go out for a bit?"

Ty didn't even look up as he said, "You know I don't care if you go out."

Her eyebrows drawing in, she blurted out, "You don't?" Her parents would definitely care if she went out randomly without saying where she was going, with whom, and why.

But Ty clearly wasn't about that, judging by the frown he turned towards her. "No? You know the deal. Tell me if you're staying overnight somewhere and send me a four if you need me."

Send him a...? That made no sense. Val simply shook her head and left. It would have been easier to run away from the apartment if Sam's pants weren't so tight. Instead she was stuck with an awkward shuffle. She wished she'd changed, but it was too late. Plus, if she were lucky, they would meet up, switch bodies, and she would never have to talk to Sam again.

It didn't take long to get to the school and when she got there, she was relieved that no one else was hanging around on a Sunday evening. But then, where was Sam?

"Val."

She nearly jumped out of her skin at the sound of her own voice. Whirling around, she put a hand to her chest. There he was, in her comfy clothes and... Well, her hair was a little mussed, but it looked like he hadn't done anything to her body while she wasn't around.

"Sam!"

She rushed over and took hold of her own arms while he frowned at her. She felt her arms and patted her hair down, but when she moved her hands farther down her body, he pushed her away.

"What are you doing?" he asked irritably.

"Making sure my body is alright. What does it look like?"

"It looks like you're feeling me up." He rolled his eyes and took another step away. "Now, what are we supposed to do about this?"

Startled, she shook her head. "How am I supposed to know that?"

He shrugged. "You're the smartest kid at school. I thought maybe you'd have some answers or...something."

The compliment felt nice, but it didn't help. She looked at the sunset, which sent pink and purple rays across the sky just beyond the school. Nothing she'd learned in that building could help them now.

"I'm not that kind of smart," she muttered.

"Sure, you are," he said softly. "You're super duper smart. I'm sure you've got something in…*here*?" He touched his head. "Or…*there*." He pointed to her head. "Somewhere. You've always got an answer."

"Do I?" she asked absently as she wrapped her arms around herself.

"Literally, always." He came closer and patted her on the shoulder. "You don't even let other people answer questions when they know the answers. So…let's find some of those answers, eh?"

Tightening her arms around herself, she narrowed her eyes at him. "What do you mean I don't let other people answer questions?"

"I mean, like, you always gotta be first." He lifted a hand in the air to demonstrate. "Because you know everything. And the teachers love that so no one else ever gets to answer the questions."

"That's *not* true."

"Val." He put his hands together into a prayer position and smiled at her. "You're focusing on the wrong thing. Just get us out of this."

"I *can't*." She threw her hands up and watched as the smile dropped from his face. *Her* smile that she didn't give out willy-nilly like he did. "I have no point of reference for *this*. There's nothing in any textbook written that would talk about *this*. *This* doesn't happen to people!"

"Well, it very clearly does," he said calmly, replacing the smile from before. "But between your brain and my, um, *something*, I'm sure we can figure this out."

Val stared at him for a moment, frowning at the unfamiliar smile on her own familiar face. "That's what you're contributing here? *Something*?"

He bit his lip and glanced at the last little rays of the sunset. "I really feel like you're focusing on the wrong thing again."

"I'm sorry," she said. She came closer and gently placed her hands on his shoulders. "You're right. Here, why don't I rip the skin off your body and try climbing into it?"

44

Grasping her elbows, he sucked in a deep breath and said, "Do you think that would work?"

"*Sam*." She shook his shoulders and pulled her elbows out of his hands. "Obviously I'm not going to rip my own skin off my own body."

Licking his lips, he looked away. When he looked back, his eyes were lit up. "Okay. Well…let's just go to Emerge then!"

"The hospital." She put a hand on her hip. "You want to go to a hospital so we can get stuck in the psych ward?"

"That won't necessarily happen."

"That will one hundred percent happen. We're not doing that. In fact, we shouldn't tell anyone because everyone will think we're crazy."

Sam seemed to deflate at her words. But she knew she was right, and he had to face that. It wasn't like they were suffering from a head cold or some other bodily ailment. As far as she could tell, the only other odd thing that that happened today was the power going out at the mall.

She snapped her fingers. "The mall! The power went out. Maybe we got zapped by something."

"Maybe…" His eyebrows drew in. "But how does that help us?"

"I don't know yet." She ran a hand over her head and then dropped her hand when she realized how soft Sam's hair was. "But maybe if we go back there tomorrow when it's open, we can find some clues."

"Okay…well… Okay."

"What?"

"The mall opens at nine. After school starts. So…"

"So we'll go to school for each other."

Sam sighed heavily and looked down at himself. She got it. She didn't want this any more than he did. "Are you sure about this?"

"No," she answered honestly. "But what choice do we have?"

"None, I guess." He shook his head. "Okay, well… Tony's going to expect to meet up with you to walk to school. And to pretty much spend all day with you. You can make something up for why you can't hang out after school. Don't tell him you're hanging out with me."

She scowled. "*Ouch*."

He tilted his head at her, his mouth softening sympathetically. "I didn't mean it that way. Just he won't understand why I would suddenly be hanging out with you at the mall."

"Yeah, alright. I get it. No one wants to hang out with me."

"Val, that's not—"

"It's fine." She flicked her wrist, knowing how petulant she sounded. "Whatever. We'll just get through the school day, go back to the mall, and get our bodies back."

"Okay," he said quietly. "See you tomorrow, then."

"Sam," she said urgently just as he turned away. When he looked back at her, she said, "Please don't dress me dumb tomorrow."

He lifted an eyebrow. "Don't dress you…dumb? What is that supposed to mean?"

"Just dress me, like—" She waved her hands in front of herself, searching for the right words. "Like normal. Normal clothes, Sam."

"Okay," he said, giving her a dead stare. "Please dress me *normal*, too."

"Do you…own any pants that aren't this tight?"

"*No.*" With that, he whirled around and stalked off, once again with her body and her comfortable clothes.

# Chapter Seven

Fooling four different families proved not to be as much of a challenge as they'd thought. Ty largely ignored Val, even when she pointedly said goodnight to him. She thought it was odd that Sam's brother didn't seem to care one iota about Sam's comings or goings or when he did what. So long as the dishes were done, right? Val gave Sam's bed one disparaging look before stripping off his too tight jeans and climbing in.

When Sam got back to the Davis home, Mr. Davis very sternly "reminded" him that he needed to tell them when he was going out. Sam, who had all but forgotten what it was like to have a parent care that much, immediately regretted not taking more care in Val's body. His guilt dissipated when he was told he'd have to clean the kitchen and then turn in early. But at least the Davises hadn't suspected a thing.

Not even when Sam found Val's bedroom, discovered it was shared with Juliette, and then turned the lights out and crawled into bed. Two minutes later, Juliette was tapping him on the shoulder and laughing about Val pulling the silliest prank ever. Of course—he was in Juliette's bed. He laughed it off and then went over to the other bed. But then Juliette commented on him sleeping in his clothes, so he had no choice but to get into Val's pyjamas. It felt like this day would never end. At least he remembered to fold up her glasses and leave them on her nightstand.

Meanwhile, Ana had gone back to Tony's house only to find both his sisters *still* talking about nonsense. At least, she'd decided to brush it off as nonsense. Maddy's voice sounded strained as Stella talked about her modeling stuff. They didn't seem to care that Ana slipped in unnoticed and went straight up to Tony's room. With nothing else to do, she'd gotten into his bed, clothes and all.

Back at the Dellagusta casa, Tony found Abuela asleep on the couch, a middle-aged man sitting at the kitchen table with a younger man, and still no dinner for Tony. Maybe he was supposed to have made his own? He was used to shared family meals that someone else made. But now these two men were looking at him like he was a nuisance. The younger one finally slid over a plate with a burrito on it toward Tony.

"You can have the last one, Anita," he said.

Tony was tempted to reject it but then his stomach grumbled. Mumbling a thank you, he picked up the plate and took it to what he assumed was Ana's room. There were posters on the walls of famous baseball players, and a jersey that looked like it would fit...well, *him*. In his current state. There was also a pair of avocado-themed shorts and t-shirt near the pillow on the bed. Figuring he had nothing else to do, he changed out of Ana's clothes and into the pyjamas, ate the delicious burrito, and tried his best to get comfortable in bed.

*     *     *

Monday morning, not a single one of them was ready to face the day. Val had really held out hope that she would wake up in her own body. Disappointed and dismayed, she quickly put on the pair of the pants she'd hastily taken off in the dark last night.

Don't dress Sam dumb? All his clothes were dumb. The shirt she'd slept in was some loose, slouchy off-the-shoulder thing. The one on the floor had *strategic* rips in it. She wasn't even sure she wanted to look in the drawers or closet, but she didn't have much choice. At least there was a normal-looking shirt with a collar in the closet. She put it on, only to feel how tight to her skin it was. Closing her eyes, she wished for this day to pass quickly.

She was supposed to meet Tony at a specific time and place, right on the corner near the apartment building. But when she got there, Tony was nowhere to be found. Tapping her foot, she looked around. This was ridiculous. She shouldn't need to wait around for a guy who wasn't even really her best friend.

A huffing sound drew her attention, and she whirled around again. There was Tony…breathing heavily like he'd just run a marathon. Only, he wasn't dressed for a marathon. He was wearing jeans that were sagging and a white t-shirt with a stain on it. His hair was mussed, and his backpack was slung over one shoulder. Val didn't know that it was Ana who hadn't taken any care with Tony's appearance today.

"Samuel," Ana wheezed.

Val lifted an eyebrow. "Anthony."

"Shall we?" Ana gestured towards the path to school.

Val nodded. "Yes. Let's."

Ana tugged on her pants, wondering why Tony didn't just buy them in a different size or put some mass on this adorably gangly body of his. She glanced at her "friend." Sam had no problem wearing tight pants.

Val did, though, and with every step, she made an awkward rotating motion with her hips in an effort to get the denim to stretch just the tiniest bit. She grunted with every effort and only stopped when Ana addressed her—or rather *Sam.*

"How was your weekend?" Ana asked, completely forgetting that Tony and Sam had literally spent nearly their entire day together yesterday.

Val didn't notice anyway. "It could have been better," she admitted. Then she tried Sam's charming smile. "I mean—it was totally fine. Dude. You should know, you were there."

"I was." Ana nodded vigorously and also tried Sam's charming smile. She had no idea how that would look on Tony, though. "Indeed. I was. And it was nice."

Val frowned as she watched Ana hike her pants up again. "Are you okay, Tony?"

"*Yes*," Ana said too quickly. "Of course. Why wouldn't I be? I'm perfectly charming in every way. Let's get to school."

Val's eyebrows lowered and she didn't say anything about the pained look on Ana's face. Or the fact that Ana kept trying to pull her pants up while she kept twisting her hips to get Sam's to loosen. If they could see themselves, they would agree—and probably laugh—that they looked quite silly. But they were both too lost in their own thoughts to care about that.

They both fell silent for the remainder of their walk to school. When they got there, neither girl knew what to do with herself. Val didn't even know where Sam's locker was; Ana did know where Tony's was, but only because it was a few lockers away from hers. Despite that, she didn't know what she'd do with his locker anyway. This was bad.

Val didn't have to wonder for too long what her next step should be. Not when she saw…*herself*. A version of herself she never thought she'd see. Ever.

Sam had put on the tightest dress she owned—a bright orange thing her free-spirited great-aunt had bought her—and paired it with black rainboots, presumably because it was cloudy outside. He'd also…done her makeup? For school? And was practically strutting down the hallway.

"Pardon me," she said anxiously as she hastily left Ana's side and rushed over to him. He smiled at her, and her scowl deepened. "Excuse me," she said, bumping him to the side of the hallway with her hip. "What are you wearing?" she hissed under her breath.

"You said don't dress you dumb," he said, his eyes widened innocently.

"I meant like dress me, like—like—not like *that!*"

"Shh…" Sam looked around, but it didn't seem like anyone was paying attention to them.

"I know, I know." She looked around, too. "You don't want anyone to see you talking to me. But seriously, *why* are you wearing that?"

"First of all—" he held a finger up "—I don't care if people see me talking to you. And second, you look great."

She looked down at herself and the jeans she'd been trying to stretch out all morning. Sam unexpectedly burst out laughing.

"No, I meant, like…*me.*" He pointed to his torso. "Me, as you. *I* look great, but *you* really pull this dress off. It's great."

"It's *hideous*. I only keep it because my auntie gave it to me." She sighed and then gestured to his face. "And where are my glasses?"

"They just didn't vibe with the dress," Sam said. Though, admittedly, it had been a bit of a challenge getting to school with Val's nearsightedness.

She huffed and pointed to the rainboots. "What—*why*, Sam?"

He held his hands up. "This is fashion, Val."

"Why does fashion have to be so *tight?*" She tugged on the belt loops of her jeans to illustrate.

He shrugged and glanced past her to his best friend—who wasn't really his best friend. "I don't know, but Tony's looking for you. Go back to him, he'll take care of you."

Tony, in fact, would not take care of Val. Because he was currently struggling to get out of Ana's house and to school on time. From the minute he'd woken up, he'd been given chore after chore. He'd barely woken up when Ana's dad had called for her—repeatedly—and Tony, dismayed, had dragged himself to the living room to him. Señor Dellagusta had shoved a full basket of laundry at him and had told him to "feed the girls" after he got that started.

Ana could have mentioned they kept chickens in the backyard. That might have helped him out that morning while he was wandering around looking for young hungry girls. Instead, Ana's brother had irritably asked Tony if he'd taken care of the chickens yet. That had clued Tony in pretty quickly, but at least it hadn't been hard to figure out where the feed was.

Unfortunately, everything was made ten times worse by the constant nagging pain somewhere in his lower midriff. He could have begged off. Maybe he should have. But he made a plan, a promise really, that he'd do Ana's thing until they could figure this out. And apparently that meant enduring whatever condition *this* was.

He'd barely made it out of the house without more chores piled onto him and only realized halfway through his walk to school that he hadn't even tried to look for a lunch he could bring. Not that he thought he could stomach any food right now.

When he got to the school and the first thing he saw was a very dressed-up Val talking to Sam, he rubbed his eyes, wondering if he hadn't gotten enough sleep last night. But no. It was them. If he were in his own body, he would absolutely go over to them and rib them for…whatever it was they were doing together. In fact, he was *very* interested to know what they could possibly be doing. But he didn't have the time to find out. School was about to start, and he still had to find Ana.

It took him a moment to remember to look for *himself*. When he did see her, he rolled his eyes. Ana was tugging on his pants like no one's business.

He approached her from behind and said, "You ever hear of a belt?"

Ana jumped and then whirled around, her eyes narrowed. "Don't *do* that to me, Cleaver."

"Sorry, Dellagusta. But seriously." He gestured to her attire. "What are you doing? Put on a belt next time."

"Oh, there won't be a next time. I'm getting that body back today."

"Eh...speaking of your body—"

"*What?*"

"We're going to see a doctor after school."

Ana's whole face scrunched up. "I'm not going to your doctor's appointment. I don't want to do that whole...turn your head and cough thing."

Tony rolled his eyes almost out of his head. "Not for *me*. For *you*. For *this* body." He gestured to himself.

"Why, what'd you do to it?"

He clutched a hand to his chest. "*I* didn't do anything to it. I found it like this!"

"Oh." Her face softened as she glanced down at his stomach. "That."

"*Yeah.*"

"Did you try what I suggested?" she asked in a soft voice.

He frowned in thought. "Lie down? I was lying down all night. Was that supposed to help?"

"Maybe," she said lightly.

Tony scoffed at her but didn't get a chance to retort when the bell rang. "You know what? Whatever. Let's just get through this day and then we can figure out how to get you your broken body back so you can go home to your broken family and never talk about this again."

Ana's breath caught in her throat. He didn't have to be rude about her. *Or* her family. There was nothing wrong with either of them. "Fine," she spit out before spinning away from him.

She was rejoined by Val and the two girls—very much looking like boys but not acting like them—walked side-by-side into the school.

# Chapter Eight

After exchanging schedules, Val felt a modicum of relief knowing it wouldn't be too hard to get through Sam's classes. They were lower level, and though they didn't share any, she figured if she needed him, she knew where to find him. Provided, of course, that he went to her own classes.

What did bother her, however, was just how many people talked to her throughout the day. It was like Sam had friends in every class, every hallway, across the schoolyard even. Lots of girls said a more-than-friendly hello to "Sam" and the less Val acknowledged them, the more they seemed to like it! And despite not being a part of any of the sports teams at all, it felt like all the athletes were friends with him, too.

Val was exhausted by the time lunch came around. And even then, she could hardly get a moment's peace. She was almost relieved to see Tony sitting at a table by himself in the cafeteria.

Except it wasn't Tony. It was Ana. Ana, who had gone through Tony's morning classes in a state of absolute confusion. Creative Writing 201? She hadn't even known there was a 101, and she wasn't creative or a writer. And his politics class was so boring she'd nearly fallen asleep.

On top of that, she didn't really know who Tony's crowd was. He wasn't unpopular, but it seemed he was close to the artsy, nerdy, and band kids. *Not* the female athletes that Ana kept mistakenly saying hello to out of habit. Every time she did, they gave her a weird look and brushed her off.

Angela, one of the gymnasts who was in Ana's gym class, did stop when Ana said hi to her, however. She slowed her gait, looked Ana up and down, and literally backtracked with a sweet smile on her face. That's when Ana knew she'd made a horrible mistake.

"Hey, Tony," Angela cooed, her bright green eyes shining. "Did you change your mind?"

"Uh…about what?" Ana asked.

"Me." Angela's smile widened, and she stepped closer. "It's okay. I forgive you for not asking for a second date." She reached out and took Ana's hand. "You can do it now."

"I…" Ana looked down at their hands before slowly slipping hers out of Angela's loose grasp. Not only did she not want to have this conversation for Tony, but she also did *not* want to set Tony up with Angela. Ever. "I was just saying hi, Angela. That's all."

Angela's mouth dipped into a frown. "Fine. Play hard to get." She turned on her heel and walked away, leaving Ana…something. She wasn't going to say she was jealous, because that was crazy.

Instead, she went to the cafeteria and sat at a table, waiting for Sam to arrive. Of course, Val came in his place, plopping down across from Ana. Val shifted in her chair, pulling at her tight jeans. Ana, similarly, was squirming to get hers to sit just right. Neither of them knew what to say to the other.

In fact, when Ana did finally decide to speak up to ask how Val's day was going, Val tersely answered, "It's fine. Why would you ask that?"

"I don't know," Ana quickly replied. "I just thought we'd talk about our days or…something."

"Mine's fine." Val, remembering she was supposed to be best friends with Tony, gave Ana a tight smile. "How is yours going?"

Ana now realized the pitfall in having insisted on conversing with her supposed best friend. Her day was going horribly but she couldn't say that to "Sam" without having a proper explanation to support it. She smiled, too, and said, "Just great. Angela asked me out."

"Oh." Val was genuinely surprised at that. Tony didn't seem like Angela's type.

"Yeah… Do you think I should go out with her?"

"Uh…" What would Sam say? Was he shallow enough to suggest Tony should say yes to any pretty girl who came along? Or should she tell the truth? Trying for a bit of both, she said, "You can if you want. She's a bit snooty but I guess she's okay."

"Snooty?" Ana had never known Angela to be snooty. Maybe she acted like she was better than some of the other girls on her team…and the other athletes. But she was just confident! "Well…okay, then I won't go out with her if it would bother you."

"No, it doesn't bother *me*," Val said, truly not caring who Tony went out with.

"If you say so…" Not that Ana *wanted* to go out with one of her friends. Oh, this was messed up. Why had she even brought it up?

"I really don't care," Val said truthfully.

"Good." Ana nodded. "Let's just stop talking about it."

"Agreed."

*     *     *

While these two would-be best friends shared a sullen and quiet meal together, Sam and Tony struggled without each other. Tony never realized just how much he relied on Sam's extroversion to navigate the ups and downs of high school relationships. But in Ana's body, he didn't even know where his relationships lay.

His own friends would never look Ana's way—mostly because female athletes were intimidating to them—and he caught glimpses of them throughout the day, trying to interact with Ana. He had no idea who Ana hung out with, other than the other baseball players. But they seemed to all act coolly towards him and he couldn't figure out why. Maybe he was doing something wrong or had broken some unspoken social girl code. Maybe it would take him forever to figure that out in Ana's body.

Sam, on the other hand, was hurting for good company. He couldn't find a friend no matter where he went. Companionship was his greatest asset, but in Val's body, no one would talk to him. If only Val hadn't spent her school career building an island of herself, maybe one or two people would talk to him. But the only people who acknowledged him were the teachers. Oh, how he missed Tony.

He had tried once or twice just to say hi to Tony and had been brushed off. That hurt, but if Sam knew the truth was because Ana was in Tony's body, he would have understood—and been there to help Ana.

He did, however, get some unwanted attention due to his choice in clothing for the day. Particularly from Daniel, the second smartest person in their grade. After the long and gratuitous look Daniel had given Sam from the first moment he'd seen him that morning, Sam had been avoiding him. He'd tried to ignore the many more glances Daniel had sent him, all the while wondering if there was something more going on between Daniel and Val that Sam didn't know about.

And why would he? He and Val weren't exactly friends, and Val was a pretty closed-off person. Private, yes, and also just didn't interact very often with her classmates. Sam didn't know that was because Val had no idea how to relate to her classmates. He assumed it was because she thought she was better than everyone else.

So it stood to reason that she might have something going on with Daniel, but that she wasn't open about it. Sam's worst fears came true when Daniel sat with him at lunch, a smile on his face, and said, "Hey, Valerie, you look great today."

"Thanks," Sam said automatically. He had, after all, put a lot of thought into Val's outfit. And he *did* look great as her.

Daniel looked away and then back at Sam. "Okay, so...without your glasses, you can't see me well enough to know it's Daniel, I'm guessing."

"I know it's you," Sam said irritably. "Why would you say that?"

"Because you haven't insulted me yet today," Daniel said with laughter in his voice.

"Oh." Sam took a good look at him and responded with, "That's seriously the worst shirt I've ever seen on someone with your body shape." He wasn't wrong either. The plain brown t-shirt with a breast pocket was completely the wrong size and shape for him.

Daniel frowned and proceeded to take out his lunch, much to Sam's chagrin. "Not your usual type of insult, but okay. What are you doing after the debate?"

Sam didn't want to do Val's debate, so what he was doing afterwards was a moot point. And besides, what did Daniel care what Val was doing after? "Why...?"

"Well, because... *I'm* not doing anything after. So, I thought if you're not, then..." Daniel bobbed his eyebrows. "Maybe we can do nothing...together?"

The light finally dawned for Sam and he almost laughed out loud. So, there was nothing going on between Val and Daniel, but that didn't stop Daniel from asking. "Wait, are you...are you trying to ask me out?"

"Yes?"

"Have you ever actually...asked someone out before?"

Daniel's eyebrows puckered as the corners of his mouth dipped down. "*Yes*. Lots of times."

"Successfully?" Sam blurted out.

"Wow." Daniel plopped the lid on his sandwich container back on and shoved it back into his lunch bag. "I know we're academic rivals, but I didn't think you'd be like this outside of debate club." He stood up and gave Sam a severe frown. "And to think I always defended you whenever people called you an ice queen. But you really are one. Ugh."

Sam opened his mouth to defend himself. He certainly *wasn't* an ice queen. But, on the other hand, Val kind of was. Even he had called her that before. If she'd wanted him to preserve her reputation, he'd done a fine job of it.

*     *     *

School was bad enough, but going home to fake homes was even worse. They were familiar with Bridgetown High, but none of them knew what to expect afterwards. When Tony got home, he found Abuela, but Ana's dad and brother were gone and there was still no sign of her mom. On top of that, Abuela told Tony she was hungry. And though Tony could understand—having been taking Spanish class at school—he had no idea how to communicate with her to see what she actually wanted. He didn't even try, and instead found some leftovers to warm up for her. She made a face when he brought it to her but didn't audibly complain. The whole time, Tony's back and stomach hurt so much he could barely move. He ended up lying down for the rest of the evening, waiting for sweet sleep to take him.

When Sam got back to Val's place, he was relieved to find it was Mr. Davis's turn to cook dinner. But that meant Sam had to take the dog out. It was a chore he was more than happy to do. The dog, however...not so much. Shadow was incredibly apprehensive about Sam, and Sam suspected he knew "Val" wasn't quite herself. Still, Sam managed to convince the dog to go out with him, and he even cleaned up after him. After dinner, he discovered that it was family game night, and the chosen game was Scrabble. Oh, if only Val had switched bodies with Tony. Tony would have killed it. Instead, Sam "let" Mrs. Davis win, and they all thanked him for not playing to the best of his abilities.

Val would have never given up the win, however. She was competitive everywhere she went, including with her family. She used to go a little easier on Juliette and Harrison, until one time Harrison had gloated over a Settlers of Catan win that he hadn't technically rightfully earned. Ever since then, if her siblings wanted to win, they would have to step up. But now she was stuck with Sam's brother, who didn't seem like he'd be interested in doing anything with her, let alone play a board game. Maybe a video game, if all the consoles at the TV were any indication. But Val wasn't exactly in the mood— or the right body—for that.

When Ana got to Tony's house, she foraged for snacks like her life depended on it. And maybe it did. Tony's body had a surprisingly voracious appetite. She'd almost forgotten what it was like to eat a large meal and not feel sick to her stomach afterward. So she gathered as much as she felt like having and snuck off to Tony's room before any of his family could find her and stop her.

# Chapter Nine

The next morning, they were all unsurprisingly disappointed to find themselves in someone else's body. Val, who was thoroughly uncomfortable with both the body and the clothing that belonged to it, rummaged through Sam's clothes for something more comfortable. She did find a pair of grey sweats that she paired with a black hoodie and tank top underneath. That would do for today.

She met Ana at school, still unaware that she wasn't Tony, and noticed she'd put a belt on her loose pants. She'd also put on a blue dress shirt that made Tony's blue eyes pop. Val complimented the shirt, because she figured that was something Sam would say to Tony.

Ana's eyes grew large as she took in Val's appearance. "Sam..." she whispered, leaning in. "Why are you dressed so...*hot?*"

"What?" Val backed away. "Are you crazy? It's just sweat pants."

"*Grey* ones." Ana pushed her sleeves up while rolling her eyes.

"Okay, you're one piece away from business casual," Val retorted. "And put your forearms away. No one needs to see that."

Ana pulled the sleeves back down and gave Val one last look. "See you in free period?"

"Sure."

Their mornings weren't nearly as awful as either girl had expected. Val aced Sam's English test on Shakespeare's *Macbeth*, did his math homework for him before class even ended, and somehow managed to while away the time during his art class. But she hadn't been prepared for just how many girls would compliment her appearance. In sweats! Teenagers were crazy, in her opinion.

Ana, despite yesterday's snag, didn't have much of a problem pretending to be Tony. She half-listened during chemistry, didn't fall asleep during sociology, and accidentally got a perfect score on his Spanish quiz. She hadn't even known Tony was taking Spanish, but it was a happy little surprise for her.

During their free period—because why wouldn't besties choose the same free period—the two girls met up in the library. Neither one quite knew what to say to the other beyond "How is your day going?" Of course, if they'd been honest, they would have admitted their days were each going…weirdly. But not…as terrible as yesterday. Just not great.

Val did admit to Ana that wearing the grey sweatpants had been a poor decision. Ana jokingly offered to switch pants with her, and it was the first time Val felt like laughing since the switch. Or maybe even in the last few weeks.

They were quietly wasting away the time, minding their own business when the school librarian, Mr. Pfizer, approached them. He looked a little uncomfortable—wringing his hands together and frowning—but didn't stop until he'd reached the table where Val and Ana were.

"Sam, Tony, er…" Mr. Pfizer's frown deepened. "I'm sorry but the principal's asked to see you both in his office. Right now."

Ana, who'd spent plenty of time in the office for a plethora of nonsense reasons, immediately rose, though she gave a little sigh. But Val remained where she was and scowled.

"*Why?*" Val asked, her tone of voice stopping Ana in her tracks. "Did we do something wrong?"

"Um, well—"

"Mr. Pfizer," Ana said with urgency in her voice. Was she about to get in trouble for Tony's delinquency? "*Did* I do something wrong?"

The librarian's hands started to wring even faster. "You just need to go see Principal Santini, okay? He'll explain everything."

Val exchanged an irritated look with Ana. If Tony had gotten them in trouble, she'd be annoyed. But if Sam was the culprit… Well, he'd be hearing about *that* after school. She certainly wouldn't be serving detention for him. Val's frown deepened, but she picked up her backpack, rose, and led the way out of the library.

Once they were on their way, Val hissed, "What'd you do?"

"I don't know," Ana whispered back. "I was going to ask you the same thing."

Why did boys have to be so frustrating? Ana could handle a "heart-to-heart" with Principal Santini in her own body because she pretty much always found a way to talk herself out of getting into too much trouble. But she had no idea what Tony would even get in trouble for, let alone how she'd deal with it.

Val stomped ahead of Ana all the way to the office. When she got in, she smiled at Mrs. Robertson, remembered it was Sam's gorgeous smile, and immediately frowned again. "Principal Santini wants to see us?"

Mrs. Robertson gingerly grabbed the delicate frame of her tortoiseshell glasses that were hanging on a chain around her neck and put them on. She peered at the computer screen in front of her and hemmed and hawed a couple of times. "Ah, yes. Yes, he does. Go on in, boys."

Once again, Val and Ana caught each other in an uneasy gaze. But they bravely stepped through Mr. Santini's door. When he saw them come in, he gave them a smile and motioned to the two club chairs in front of him.

"May I ask why we're here?" Val said, without sitting.

"Of course, Sam." Mr. Santini once again gestured to the chairs. Ana was already sitting in one. When Val finally reluctantly sat, he said, "A couple of your teachers are concerned about the grades you got on your tests today."

Ana's eyebrows drew in. "What do you mean?"

"Well...I've never heard of either of you having this problem," Santini said. "But it would appear that, uh—well, it seems as though you've both cheated today."

"*What?*" Val stood up so quickly the chair squeaked back a few inches. She didn't even care if she was in Sam's body and she'd taken Sam's test. She was insulted anyone would accuse her of cheating. "I've never cheated once in my life."

"I have no idea what you're talking about," Ana said. "I can't even remember— *Ay, caramba...*"

"Yeah." Santini, ignoring Val's outburst, turned his attention to Ana. "You've been getting a steady C plus in Spanish all semester. Until today. Congrats on the perfect score, but Señorita Lacosta is still...concerned."

"Well, what about me?" Val asked, not even bothering to give Ana a chance to defend herself. "I didn't cheat on anything."

"Sam..." Santini sighed. "I mean you no disrespect but you're not... Well... You've never once done so well on an English test, let alone one on Shakespeare. I know you try your best, but Mr. Deacon said you turned in your test first *and* got ninety-nine percent."

"Where did I lose a mark?" popped out of Val's mouth before she could stop herself.

"Wait, so you're mad that I—uh, that *we* studied for once?" Ana said. "You're joking, right?"

"We're not mad," Santini said evenly. "The teachers are just…surprised."

"You can't prove we cheated," Val said, crossing her arms and sitting back down. "You wouldn't find any proof anyway. At least not for me."

"Or me," Ana said quickly.

Steepling his fingers in front of him, Mr. Santini asked, "Would you boys mind showing me your phones?"

Ana's breath caught in her throat. She certainly hadn't cheated, but if Santini looked at her phone, he might find a very *odd* conversation…with "Ana." Val, of course, was in the same position. But she wasn't about to be bullied into giving away her secret.

"Yes, I would," Val said confidently. "You can't ask to see our phones. Those are personal property and private to us. Plus, I didn't even have my phone with me during class."

"Neither did I," Ana said truthfully. She hadn't needed it and therefore had left it in Tony's locker. It was Tony's anyway and she didn't want to go on it more than she absolutely had to. But Santini wouldn't understand that. "You can tell Señorita Lacosta I studied with Ana Dellagusta this weekend because I was tired of failing her class."

Mr. Santini's eyebrows rose but before he could answer, Val said, "Yeah… And I just wanted to do well for once. So."

She shrugged and together, she and Ana got up and left without being dismissed. Mr. Santini didn't try to stop them, nor did he even bother to call out to them. Val grumbled as they walked away from the office. She'd lost most of her free period doing nothing and then *that*. She had things to prepare for but without Sam around, she would never be able to do that.

The debate meet was on Saturday. It was Tuesday. Somehow, she had to get ready for it...*and* get her body back before then. But she would have a hard time doing that if Tony dragged her down.

Putting her hand on Ana's arm, Val stopped and waited for Ana to turn to her. "Did you cheat on your Spanish test?"

Ana scowled so hard, the muscles in her cheeks twitched. "*No.*"

"Are you sure? Principal Santini said you were getting Cs..."

"Sam." Shrugging off Val's hand, Ana put her fists on her hips. "Come on. If anyone was cheating...it was you. It's not exactly a secret you're not an A student."

"Hey!" Val said before she could stop herself. While that may have been true of Sam, Val was still offended. "I didn't cheat and I'm not going to be dragged down by a liar, Tony."

"I didn't cheat, okay?" Ana shrugged again. But then she thought about it. Technically...if she had given Tony those answers, it would have been considered cheating. "At least, not exactly... It wasn't cheating."

Val's jaw dropped open. "Anthony Cleaver, what did you do?"

"I..." Ana took a deep breath and blurted out, "Am *not* Anthony Cleaver."

Val slowly closed her mouth, opened it silently, then closed it again as her mind reeled. "You're...not?" she whispered.

"No. And I know that's hard to believe but it's tr—"

"I'm not Sam," Val said, unabashedly cutting Ana off.

"Okay..." Ana lowered her arms and took a step closer to Val. Though the hallway was empty, the bell could ring at any moment, and they'd be swarmed by students who didn't need to hear this conversation. "I wasn't done speaking but, okay, we'll do your thing. You're not Sam?"

"No."

"And I'm not Tony."

"No."

"So…who *are* you?"

"Valerie Davis. You?"

"Ana Dellagusta."

"*Oh*. Well, that explains the…not not cheating."

"Yeah. Same here." Ana rolled her eyes. "Were you two also arguing in the middle of the mall during a power outage?"

Val nearly choked on her reply, which was a gasping "Yes." The bell rang and she looked around, startled.

Ana's eyes widened. "Let's go get our bodies!"

They split up, determined to find the boys quickly and rejoin, hoping that being together might jolt something and send them back to where they belonged.

Unfortunately, the boys hadn't had nearly as smooth a day as the girls had.

Having learned his mistake yesterday, Sam had toned down his clothes, opting for the boring slacks and unshapely sweater that Val loved so much. Just because they never interacted at school didn't mean he'd never noticed how much more she could be doing for her beautiful body. But considering how unhappy she'd been with the dress—and Daniel's reaction to it—Sam decided to just try harder to be more like Val.

Tony had slept a long time and still woken up feeling utterly exhausted. He couldn't focus on any of Ana's classes, her teachers, or her friends. All he could think about was the pain emanating through *her* abdomen. How could she live like this? And forget gym class—he could barely walk, let alone run and play dodgeball, or whatever it was they did in gym.

And so, when Ana went to the outside track where the rest of her gym class was supposed to be today, she was alarmed to not find Tony there. A couple of the other girls giggled as they passed her, but she stopped them quickly.

"Sarah, Amy." When they turned to her, looking mildly unimpressed, she asked, "Have you seen Ana?"

"Oh, I think she went to see the nurse," Amy said with a shrug.

As the two girls continued on their way, Ana stifled a groan. He *would* skip out on her gym class to see the nurse. Well, two could play that game. Putting on a pronounced limp, Ana made her way to the office. As soon as she got to the nurse, she called out, "Nurse Sanchez!"

"Just a minute, dear," came Ms. Sanchez's voice from behind a pale yellow curtain. She lowered her voice just enough that Ana could tell she was whispering to someone else. It didn't take long to figure out who. Tony was here.

"How do you rate the pain on a scale of one to ten?"

"Ten. Eleven if I could."

Ana rolled her eyes. It wasn't *that* bad, but if she barged in now, Sanchez would just throw her out. Ana impatiently waited while Sanchez got some medicine for Tony before sending him on his way. That was when Sanchez found out just how close Ana had been lurking.

"Can I help you, young man?" Ms. Sanchez said, peering at Ana over the tops of her severe glasses.

"Nope." Ana grabbed Tony's elbow. "Just looking for Ana. Come on, Ana, we have stuff to do."

"Be gentle with her," Sanchez said, her face drawn together sternly. "She's feeling quite unwell."

That gave Ana pause. She had no idea the school nurse would be that sympathetic towards her. "I will."

Ana led Tony out of the office while he clutched his stomach. "Seriously, Tony?" she hissed under her breath. "What were you thinking?"

"I just don't want to die in this body..." he moaned.

"You won't die," she said, exasperated. "Look, we have other things to worry about. Come with me."

"Where are we going?"

"To find your best friend."

Tony's best friend was currently trying not to doze off at Val's debate team meeting. He'd been avidly avoiding Daniel after yesterday's proposition, and now Daniel was acting like Val wasn't even there. Which, when Sam thought about it, was true. And kind of hilarious. Sam had to try hard to focus on the discussion and not laugh at his inner thoughts. There were four other people on the team aside from Val and each of them was going to present to the others. Right now. Which Sam was unprepared for.

"Valerie, did you want to go first?" the very sweet Carmeline asked.

"Uhhh... No."

Everyone stared at Sam as he tried to come up with any lie or excuse that would help him out. Daniel made a snarky comment, which Sam ignored. He wouldn't play that game with Val's teammates. Thankfully, the door burst open, saving him from having to answer. Unfortunately, it was Val, looking like a half-deranged version of himself as she called out her own name.

"Sorry, guys, but I have to borrow Val for...an indefinite period of time. Don't worry, she's good for the meet."

"Uh..." Sam rose while the others stared awkwardly at him. "Yup, good for the meet. Bye."

Sam rushed away and as soon as the door closed, he frowned at her attire and asked why she'd pulled him out of her own debate club meeting.

"Well, first of all—" she paused and looked behind her, as if to make sure none of them had followed "—there's no way you would have made it through that meeting unscathed. Second, we've got an...interesting problem."

"More interesting than our current problem?"

"Just follow me."

It wasn't hard for Sam to follow Val when she'd literally taken his elbow and was guiding him through the school to the west doors, which hardly anyone ever used. But he was confused and stopped short when he saw Tony and Ana waiting for them on the other side.

"What's...going on?" Sam asked slowly.

Val stood next to Ana, and they both folded their arms across their chests. But then Ana dropped hers to push up her sleeves once again and Val rolled her eyes at her.

"We all switched bodies," Val said, figuring it'd be better to rip the Band-aid off. "I'm Valerie."

"And I'm Ana."

Sam and Tony gave each other sharp looks. Then Sam let out a snicker and Tony cracked a grin. Soon enough, both boys had dissolved into a fit of giggles that they couldn't control even if they wanted to. Val once again rolled her eyes as her gaze met Ana's. How unfortunate that they'd been stuck with the school's two biggest goofballs.

# Chapter Ten

"Are they *serious* right now?" Ana asked in the most contemptable voice to ever come out of Tony's mouth.

"I'm gonna wake up any second," Val said as she stared at the two boys-turned-girls. "I just know it."

"I'm sorry," Tony said, mirth still clinging to his voice. "That makes so much sense! I mean, it's no wonder everyone keeps talking about how Val was dressed yesterday."

Sam let out another loud burst of laughter. "Didn't I look amazing? I wouldn't know, though. I can't see a thing without Val's glasses."

"Oh, no-ho-ho." Tony slapped the side of Sam's arm. "That was a poor decision on your part."

"*Tell* me about it," Val grumbled. "Seriously, Sam, can't you—"

"You probably should have tried a ponytail, though, Tony." Sam reached out and gingerly touched Tony's long silky locks.

"I would have, but—*oh*." Tony clutched his stomach again and groaned. "I know they say laughter is the best medicine, but this is killing me."

Sam's smile immediately fell, and he stepped closer to his friend. "What's wrong with you?" He glared at Ana, who had taken over Tony's body. "What's wrong with him?"

"He's *fine*," Ana drawled exaggeratedly. "It's just my period. He'll survive."

"Are you sure about that?" Sam asked as he gently patted Tony's back.

"Of course." Ana gestured to Val. "You know what I'm talking about, right?"

"Um, well…" Val scratched the back of her neck as she watched Tony groan in pain once again. She didn't know him well enough to tell if he was faking or exaggerating, but Sam seemed overly concerned. "Yeah, but not like *that*."

"Look." Ana sighed. "Can we stop talking about my period? We have bigger things to worry about." She gestured between themselves. Tony straightened up and even Sam looked like he was trying to take things more seriously. Val was glad they finally seemed to want to fix this.

"Well?" Sam shrugged.

Val turned to him, giving her plain clothes a onceover. "Well, what are we going to do?"

He let out a humourless laugh. "I'm not the smart one in this group so what exactly do you want from me? I could honestly hang out like this a little longer."

"I couldn't…" Tony said weakly. "Please, Sam."

"Well, of course we're gonna figure this out, Tony," Sam said softly as he put his hand on Tony's admittedly very strong and feminine shoulder. "Wow."

Tony looked up with miserable eyes. "What?"

"Ana's got a lot of muscles."

"I know." Tony flexed his right arm. "That's probably why she thinks she can handle this pain, but I definitely can't."

Ana slapped her own shoulder. "You *guys*. Tony, give me that back."

When Tony just lifted an eyebrow she grabbed her arm and tugged hard. Tony's body wasn't exactly muscular, and Ana was fairly steady on her feet. But in each other's bodies, Ana was able to pull him so far that he ended up collapsing into her arms and knocking her down with him. As they groaned in unison, Val put her face in her hand.

"Anyone else..." she mumbled. "I could have been in this situation with *anyone,* and it had to be you three."

Sam shot her a dirty look as he reached down first to Ana, being used to helping Tony off the ground. But he quickly remembered and moved his hand just out of Ana's reach at the last second to grab Tony's wrist. He hefted Tony up and left Ana to fend for herself while he whirled to face Val.

"And what exactly is that supposed to mean?" he asked her.

"You know..." Val waved her hand around in their directions. "Lost in her sports, lost in his books, lost in his own face."

Sam scoffed hard, Ana scowled, but Tony just kind of nodded like he couldn't help but acquiesce. When Sam elbowed him, Tony just shrugged.

"She's not, wrong, Sunny," Tony said. "You kind of do get lost in your face. And look what you did with *someone else's.*"

"Val looks great." Sam eyed Val who was wearing *his* grey sweatpants. "And I didn't even have to try that hard."

Val shook her head, put a hand on her hip, and half turned away. "You're unbelievable, Samuel. We have *things* to do."

"Oh, like what?" He tossed his hands up. "Finding people to argue with?"

Val's face flushed and she knew with Sam's colouring it would be terribly obvious. In a quiet voice, she said, "I have a debate tournament this weekend."

Sam pressed his lips together as he glanced briefly at Ana—who he forgot was Ana—and then found Tony's dancing eyes. "So...finding people to argue with?"

Tony snorted and Val shot him a sharp glare. "It's *not* like that."

"It kind of is," Ana said lightly.

"Oh, and what's Dellagusta up to this week?" Val asked. "Hitting a ball and then running around to some stupid little squares on the ground while people shout at you?"

Ana's eyes widened. "Oh, no, my game!" She grabbed Tony's shoulder and shook him. "Tony, I have a game on Saturday!"

"Oh, you're not going to that." He looked at Val and said, "I have a thing. Remember, the thing?"

Val stared at him blankly. "You say that as if I know what your thing is."

"Oh." Tony turned to Sam instead. "My thing, Sam."

"I'm afraid to ask," Ana said slowly, "but what exactly are you two doing on Saturday that you need *our* bodies for?"

Sam and Tony, having finally figured out who was who, shared an uneasy glance. Sam said, "I have a photoshoot on Saturday."

"And I'm doing a…" Tony swallowed and stared at the ground. "A live reading at my writer's group. I've put it off three times so I really can't this time."

"No *way*," Val said vehemently.

"If I wanted to read your book, I'd wait till it was out and on sale," Ana said, her eyes narrowed towards Tony.

"I am *not* missing my tournament for a-a-a *photoshoot!*" Val said the word like she'd been asked to drink poison.

"Not in my grey sweatpants, you're not," Sam said.

Val growled and stomped up to Tony, who shrank away from her in fear. "Can you *please* get him to be serious? Or do you want to be stuck in her body, too?"

Tony put a hand up to his chest and leaned even farther away. "I have *never* heard Sam speak to me like that."

"Well, either get used to it or help me get out of this stupid body." Val clenched her fists as irritation continued to rise up inside her.

"Now, Valerie." Tony tilted his head and finally stopped inching away. "Sam's not stupid, and lots of girls enjoy his body." Sam groaned and put his face in his hands while Ana snorted. Tony's eyes widened when he realized just how that sounded. "I didn't mean— Just that they— Everyone likes Sam. Get over yourself, Val."

"Are you people done?" Ana said. "Let's figure out how to fix this so I can go to my game this weekend. As *me*. I can't run with these spindly legs."

"They're not…*that* spindly," Tony muttered.

Sam put his hand on Tony's arm and said, "Don't worry, we'll get your nerdy body back." Tony just sighed, but Sam wasn't done. "And we'll get Val's nerdy body back, and Ana… You *do* have really muscular arms. Are you the slugger?"

Ana gave him a miserable look. "I'm the ace."

Sam cringed. He loved Tony with all his heart, but Tony couldn't throw a ball—any sort of ball—to save his life. "Okay, let's get Ana's body back to her, eh?"

Val looked at Tony, glancing up and down his borrowed body, and said, "Do you have any idea what they're talking about?"

He shook his head. "No, but I like the sounds of getting our bodies back. What's the plan?"

Dead silence followed his question. Of course, no one had an answer. Something like this was practically unheard of…except maybe in fiction.

Tony snapped his fingers. "I'm going to poke around some lit resources, see what I can come up with."

"*Literature?*" Val shook her head. "Never mind that. I'm going to find some *actual* sources and go from there."

"Actual sources," Tony mumbled, rolling his eyes. "Okay, have fun looking for nothing."

"Well, while you do that, I guess we'll…" Ana gave Sam some side eye "find something to do with ourselves. Like find Val's glasses."

"Oh, *thank you*," Val said emphatically. She grabbed Tony's arm. "Come on, let's get going. We'll meet up with you two later."

"Val…" Sam put his hand on Val's shoulder as she turned away. This isn't the worst thing in the world, you know."

Val's jaw clenched in a way Tony recognized, though he hadn't seen Sam that angry in a long time. She spun around, tossing Tony around in the process, so she could face Sam again. "Go home and do something, *anything* useful in my body. And get rid of that dress you wore yesterday."

Sam swallowed hard and nodded. "Yes, ma'am," he said in a resigned, disappointed way.

Val huffed and turned again, her iron grip never leaving Tony's arm. He had no choice but to follow her, though he did give Ana and Sam one more backwards glance. Once they'd gone back inside the school, Ana let out a long breath.

"Oh, man…"

"What?" Sam said.

"Nothing." Ana looked at him again and smiled. "Okay, if she's getting rid of the dress, can I have it? It's amazing! But maybe it only works on her."

Sam scoffed as he stared at her. "Are you *kidding* me? Why didn't you stick up for me if you thought that?"

She shrugged. "Val's, like, one of the prettiest girls I've ever seen, but she's *so* scary. Just very…"

"Severe."

Ana's eyes widened and so did her smile. "*Yes.*"

"That's a word I learned from Tony."

"He's a smart guy."

Sam smiled proudly. "Yeah. And she's smart, too. I'm sure they'll figure this out. Let's just go… Do *something*."

"Maybe you can show me how to get around Tony's house without getting stopped by his sisters every two seconds," she suggested.

"Oh, there's a trick to that." He took her elbow and smiled. "Come on."

"I like how you know that," she said as she walked along with him.

Smirking, Sam nudged her with his elbow. "We *are* best friends after all."

"I can't believe you two had me and Val pretending to be best friends."

"I'm sure if you tried a little harder, you *could* be best friends," he said casually.

"With…with *Val*?"

"*Yes.*" Sam glanced at the school over his shoulder as they left the grounds. He had to trust Tony could handle Val…and that Val would take care of his body. "I know she's so, like… Oh, what's the word?"

"Academic?"

"Yes! Academic. And you're so…"

"Latina?"

He rolled his eyes towards her. "I was gonna say *athletic*. You're so athletic."

"Oh, well…thanks." She lifted her hand to tuck her hair behind her ear and when she couldn't find it, she remembered—Tony's hair was much shorter than hers. She didn't want to touch Tony's hair. Instead, she looked around. They'd left the school and walked away from the core local downtown area. "Where are we going?"

"Oh." He stopped and chuckled as he looked around, too, as if he didn't even know they'd been going anywhere to begin with. "I was…heading home. But I can't go like this."

"And we can't exactly go to my place…"

He grinned. "To Tony's it is!"

He abruptly turned around while she groaned. "I thought you were joking about that. Do we have to? His sisters are awful."

Waving his hand dismissively, he picked up his pace. "They're not so bad. You'll get used to them."

"Sam…"

"Yeah."

She stopped and put her hand on his arm. In a serious voice, she said, "I don't want to get used to them. I don't want to be stuck in this body forever. There has to be a way."

Feeling how much Ana really meant it, Sam nodded and said, "I'm sure Tony and Val will figure something out."

She chewed on her lip and looked away. "You know a little something about baseball?"

Shrugging, he said, "A little. My brother and I played when we were younger. But then he ditched for football, and I had no one to sponsor me, so…"

"Oh." Her family had always found the money for her to play baseball. She couldn't linger on that, though. "Do you think *he* could play it?"

Sam's lips twitched and then he burst out laughing, clutching at his stomach. "Tony? Nooo. Seriously?" Seeing that Ana was indeed serious, he stopped laughing. "In *your* body, maybe."

"That's…that's what I meant," she said quietly. "If I don't get my body back in time, do you think you could help him play my game? It's…it's a really important game."

Sam looked into her unsmiling eyes, the exact same look Tony gave him when he needed help. How could he say no? "Sure, Ana. I'll help him. You. Both of you."

"Thank you."

# Chapter Eleven

The clacking sounds of keys being tapped in rapid succession, reverberating against the quiet, solid walls of the school library grated on Val's nerves. If she'd come to work on her debate topic, that would be different. But no— she had really agreed to research body swapping with Tony…who looked like Ana but with unbrushed hair.

Tony, however, felt comforted by the sound. It was familiar to his unfamiliar ears. And if there was anyone who could find hidden information on an obscure—and outrageous topic—it was Tony.

"Well, I never thought I'd be researching *this* one day," Tony said breathlessly as he tapped away at his keyboard.

Val hadn't touched hers yet. She didn't even know where to begin! "Why do you sound so excited?"

He shrugged. "I don't know. Stuff like this only ever happens in books and movies. It is…*a little*…exciting." He grinned at her, but she just scowled.

"Do you and Sam share the same brain cell or something?"

Choosing not to get offended, Tony leaned towards her, one finely groomed eyebrow raised high, and said, "I would think *you're* the one sharing a brain cell with Sam."

Val looked down at herself, from her decidedly masculine chest to the tight jeans, and groaned. Instead of answering him, she finally typed into the search bar on her computer: "cases, switching bodies, resolution." Three results came up, none of them particularly useful.

Meanwhile, Tony kept hemming and hawing, clicking and typing furiously. "Wow," he said every once in a while. "I see..." he mused while Val stared blankly at a ten-year-old article that seemed to have zero citations. "Oh, that's good. That's good, too."

"Tony," Val snipped. When he turned his attention to her, an innocent blank look on his face, she said, "Do you have to talk out loud like that?"

"I'm sorry," he said not sounding the least bit apologetic. "I usually do when I'm researching, but I'm usually alone when I research. Is it *bothering* you?"

*How* could he ask her that? "Yes, it is. Among *other* things."

He tilted his head, his pretty amber eyes narrowing. "Are you sure you're not just hungry? Sam's appetite is insatiable."

"Well, I..." She put a hand on her stomach as it rumbled quietly. "How did you—"

Tony's—or rather *Ana's*—smile returned. "Oh, I know my best friend."

"Good for you," she said flippantly as she turned back to her screen. "Why couldn't *you* have switched bodies with him? I'm sure you would have had a grand old time being each other. Maybe then *you* could have aced his Shakespeare test and gotten in trouble for it instead of me."

"Wait..." Laughter bubbled out of Tony, irritating Val. "*What* did you do?"

"I got a nearly perfect score on his test about Macbeth and then Ana got a perfect score on your Spanish test and we both got sent to the office for supposedly cheating. And I have never—" she turned to face him, her eyes narrowed hard "—and I mean *never* been sent to the office before."

He gaped at her. "Ana got me a perfect score? Well, my mom's gonna *love* that."

"They think you cheated, Tony!" She threw her hands up. "We couldn't explain to Principal Santini why or how we'd done so well on those tests."

"That's on you, then. If I'm stuck in this body, then I'm not in trouble."

"If you're stuck in that body, you might have a championship game to play this weekend."

His eyebrows drew in and his hand reflexively went to his stomach as another wave of pain shot through it. "Championship? I thought it was just, like, a practice or a regular game. There's no way I could play, ever, and especially not feeling like this."

An uncommon surge of sympathy swept through Val. "It can't be that bad, right? You're just exaggerating like boys do?"

"I wouldn't know," he said in a strained voice. "I've never been in a woman's body before. But if my sisters ever felt this way, I would know *that*."

"Hmm…" Val turned to her computer and positioned her hands over the keyboard. "Can you describe your symptoms?"

Tony lifted an eyebrow. "Okay…" The pain he felt was sharp and stabbing, sometimes came in waves—cramps, Val corrected—and was just intense and overwhelming.

"Tony…" she said softly. "I'm no doctor, but I think Ana's got endometriosis."

"No," he said miserably. "*I've* got it. There's gotta be something that can be done about it, right?"

"Well, yeah." She tried to smile at him, but it didn't stick. "But she…well, *you* would have to see a doctor and get assessed and be prescribed something probably."

He looked down at his borrowed body. "Why wouldn't she have done that already? She knew what I was talking about when I said I was in pain, so it's not like it's the first time."

"Maybe she has no support at home?"

"Okay, *that* makes sense." He rolled his eyes. "No one pays attention to her at home, and I doubt her dad or brother would care if she told them about this."

"How do you know that for sure?"

He shrugged. "Just a sense I got. Look, I wouldn't wish this pain on my worst enemy, but I don't have time to go see a doctor about it. I just want to get our bodies back. *Then* maybe we can convince her to get help."

Val looked doubtful but she nodded. "Okay. Did you find out anything about the…" she lowered her voice "…body swapping?"

Pushing away the pain and discomfort, he turned back to the many open tabs on his computer. "There's a ton of movies and books that reference it. We're not changelings…unless you're a troll."

"I'm not."

"We weren't cursed by anyone. I think."

"Not that I'm aware."

"Electrocution?"

"Don't think so."

"Well, that just leaves… Oh, you're not gonna like it."

She huffed impatiently. "Why? What is it?"

"Well…" He dropped his hands from the keyboard. "It could have happened when we were arguing. Some external force trying to show us what it's like to…live on the other side. Were you arguing with Sam when it happened?"

Val nodded wordlessly.

"Ana and I were arguing, too."

"How do we fix it?"

82

He shrugged. "You're the debater. You tell me."

She huffed. "I am a *debater*. Not a medical doctor, or a witch doctor, or any kind of professional. Why do you think I'd know how to fix this?"

"I don't know." He turned his hands palms up. "We talked our way into it, maybe we can talk our way out of it."

"*Talk* our way out of it? Tony, that's—"

"Wait!" Tony said excitedly. "I have one other idea, but it's even less desirable."

"Okay…"

"We'll just do each other's things and hope that breaks the curse."

Val looked down at, well, Sam's body. "What is Sam's thing?"

Tony gestured to her loosely. "Modeling. He's got that photoshoot coming up, remember?"

Her face flushing, she closed her eyes and shook her head. "Okay… So, let's try talking our way out of it."

"What's wrong, Val?" he said in a teasing tone. "Don't like having your picture taken?"

"Actually…no. I do not." She clicked a couple of times on her computer to log out and then looked at him expectantly. "Well? Let's go find our bodies and…talk our way out of this."

"I don't think that'll work," he said, taking one last lingering glance at all his tabs. Then he logged out of his computer, too. "But I'm willing to try anything to not have to feel like *this*."

For one brief moment, sympathy crossed Val's face, shining in Sam's dark brown eyes. Then she blinked rapidly and looked away. "Let's go."

As they left the library, Tony got Ana's phone and dialled his own number. When Ana answered, he was momentarily taken aback. It was almost as jarring to hear his own voice over the phone as it was to see someone else wearing his face.

"Oh, I do *not* like that," he said.

"Tony?" she whispered.

"Yeah."

"I don't like that, either."

"It's totally creepy. Where are you?"

"We went to your place."

"Ugh." Tony put a hand up to his forehead. Why had they gone *there?* "Okay, just stay put. We have an idea."

"Okay…"

Tony and Val left the school, and he led her with confident steps towards his own home. Val was quiet on the way, but judging by the way she was grinding her teeth she was either angry or anxious. Tony didn't know which, but if it were Sam making that face, he'd guess it was worry that was getting to him. He could only assume the same was true for Val.

The truth was even worse. This was the first time in Val's life where she truly didn't have an answer. No rebuttal. No solution. Just a blank space in her mind as to how this could have happened and how they were supposed to fix it.

A Tony's house, he was surprised but also relieved to see no cars in the driveway, meaning neither his parents nor his sisters would be there. He was a little less impressed when he found Sam and Ana helping themselves to the snacks in his kitchen while Sam gave her a tour of the family photos strewn about the place.

"Hello," he said in an annoyed voice as he joined them in the kitchen.

"Tony!" Ana smiled and looked him up and down. "You kept me in one piece. Good job."

He huffed and motioned to Val, who looked like she was about to scold them for being so…what? Laidback? Relaxed? Not as on edge as she was?

"I cannot believe you two are here just chilling like this," she said. So, all

84

of those things in one.

"It's *fine*, Val," Sam said, rolling his eyes. "What else were we supposed to do? Have a snack."

She sighed and sat across from him. When he slid a bag of chips towards her, she couldn't help herself. Tony was right. Sam's body was hangry. Not her, though. She was totally in control of her emotions.

"So, what's your big plan?" Ana asked, eyes shining with hope.

"Well…" Val popped a chip in her mouth. "Since we were all fighting when the switch happened, we figured if we said some nice things about each other, then maybe it'll kick us back."

Sam immediately turned to Ana and said, "Tony, you're the best friend a guy could ever ask for and I wouldn't trade you for the world."

Ana blinked at him. "That's very nice, but I'm *Ana*. We've been hanging out for the last half hour, you dork."

Tony couldn't help chuckling. "And we meant say something nice to the person you switched with. Thanks anyway, bro."

Sam shook his head. "Oh…"

"Well…" Tony turned to Val as did the other two. "This was *your* idea."

Val bit her lip. "Fine. Uh… Sam. You're the handsomest boy I've ever met."

Sam's lips parted. "Oh…okay. Um. You, uh…" He stared at her, wondering how he was supposed to follow that up. Returning the compliment, as true as it may have been, didn't seem right. "You talk good."

Val slammed her hands on the table. "*What?* That is not—"

"Shh," Tony said, lifting a hand practically in her face. "You had your turn. Ana, I can't believe you put up with this kind of pain. You're a beast."

Ana frowned and then paused a moment, thinking. "Well, I…I think you should have won that poetry contest last year."

Tony's mouth dropped open. "You…read my poem?"

"Yes." She lifted her chin. "And it was better than the winning poem."

"It certainly was *not*."

"Well, I liked your imagery better."

"Oh."

For a moment, all four of them fell silent. Tony turned to Sam and said, "Great idea, Val. It didn't even work."

Sam's eyebrows drew in for a moment before he said, "*I'm* Sam. You know that."

"Ugh!" Tony threw his hands up.

"Well, of course it didn't work," Val said. "He told me I talk good."

"You *do* talk good!"

"I *speak well*, but what does that have to do with anything?"

Sam tossed a hand in the air. "At least I put some thought into my compliment. All you ever do is practice talking! And you chose the most shallow, annoying thing to say to me. Really? Also, I don't think *handsomest* is a real word."

Anger broiled inside of Val, and she said, "It *is* a word, and—"

"Ana," Tony unapologetically cut Val off. "You could have chosen something better for me instead of bringing up *that* painful memory."

Her eyes widened. "You brought up *literal* pain, T. I am not a beast and have no desire to be. Seriously!"

Tony raised his hands in surrender, but they weren't quite done tearing each other apart. All at once, they began nitpicking at each other again. Val brought up the clothes Sam had put on, and Tony told Ana to please wear a belt so he didn't look like a dork. In response, Ana said she would look far less like a dork if she had her own body back, and Sam snipped at Val for being condescending towards him.

"Hold up!" Tony finally shouted over the chaos in his pretty voice. He held his hands up until every quieted down. "Never mind. This isn't working.

We're doing *my* plan."

"Which is?" Ana asked with ice in her voice.

"According to my sources, if we just, like, do each other's things, then everything will turn out fine." He smiled at her in a way he hoped put her at ease, but it just made her narrow her eyes as her lips turned down.

"What sources?" she asked.

After a hesitant moment, he mumbled, "*Freaky Friday*."

"As in the movie," Val said in an unimpressed tone.

Ana thought about it and then asked, "The Jodie Foster version or the Lindsay Lohan one?"

"Does it matter?" Val huffed and crossed her arms over her chest. "He wants to bet on *fiction*."

"It's better than *your* idea," Sam reminded her. "Which didn't work. And probably never will."

"Great." She gave him a fake smile. "Have fun at my debate meet while I...look pretty doing absolutely nothing."

Sam's next words got caught in his throat as Val got up. "Wait," he said, quickly rising and reaching out to take her arm. "Wait. Please. I already told Ana I'd help Tony play her game. Can't we...*all* just kind of help each other? And after this weekend, we'll seriously look into how to fix this."

Val looked at the other two, who simply shrugged in unison, and then Sam, who was imploring her with a look she would never use on anyone. But what other choice did she have? "Okay. Fine. I guess we're doing this."

# Chapter Twelve

Since they were already at Tony's house, Tony and Ana elected to stay there so they could sort out whatever would happen to them on the weekend. With a huge amount of trepidation, Sam said goodbye to Tony. Val didn't say anything as she left with him.

"Well…" Tony sat on his own bed and smoothed out the blanket that had been haphazardly tossed overtop it. He couldn't believe Ana had slept here last night but he tried not to linger on that. "What now?"

With a sigh, Ana climbed into the bed behind him and yanked out the hair tie he was wearing. He let out a little yelp, but she told him to calm down. Then with firm, quick strokes, she gathered up his hair to fix the ponytail. "You really thought you'd pass as me with your hair like *that*?"

"Do you maybe want to be serious for a minute?" He gritted his teeth as she pulled a little harder than necessary.

Quickly, she got the hair tie on and finally let him go. "For a minute, sure."

"Ana." He turned around on the bed to face her. But then he realized how close they were and that they were in his bed *together* and he scooted back. His butt went over the edge, and he nearly fell, but Ana grabbed his hands and kept him on the bed.

He was about to thank her, but the door swung open and Maddy poked her head inside. "Hey, To— Oh. Goodness. My bad. Didn't realize you had…company."

"It's not company," Tony blurted out. then he remembered that Maddy thought he was Ana. Shaking Ana's hands off his, he cleared his throat. "I mean, I'm just a friend."

Ana shifted uncomfortably, trying to create some space between them. "Yeah, it's not what it looks like."

A smile slowly grew across Maddy's face. "Are you sure? Maybe it doesn't look like what you think it looks like."

Ana and Tony gave each other confused looks and then Tony said, "What? Never mind. We're just talking. Can you leave?"

The smile disappeared from Maddy's face as her eyebrows lowered. "Excuse me, missy, but I have a right to talk to my own brother. Tony—" She focused on Ana. "Your book's dried out. But I didn't look at the inside to see if the words are legible because I know how you are. You're welcome."

She held out the water-damaged notebook and shook her hand impatiently when no one moved to get it. Finally, Ana, realizing it was her job, got off the bed and reached out for the book.

"Thank you," she said quietly.

"Uh huh." Maddy glanced surreptitiously at Tony before giving Ana a tight smile. "I'm leaving the door open."

"That's fine," Ana said with a sigh as Maddy left.

After a moment, when Tony was sure Maddy had gone far enough away, he crossed his arms and said, "Great. Now she thinks there's something going on between us."

Ana looked away, her eyes catching on a picture on the wall of Tony and

Sam from what looked like their grade 8 grad photos. They both had their cap and gown plus matching smiles. If Sam had been in the room with Tony, Maddy wouldn't have thought twice. "Is that so bad?" she whispered.

"What?"

She looked back at him. "Is it so bad that your sister thinks you're into me?"

"Ana." His eyes and voice serious, he tilted his head at her. "I'm literally *in* you right now."

She rolled her eyes. "Ugh, don't say it that way. Come on, Sam said you would learn to pitch for me."

She hopped off the bed, but he grabbed her wrist. "Wait, Ana. The book?"

She held it out to him and with gentle hands he took it. When he opened it up, his heart lurched. The words were…mostly readable. But it felt like his very soul had fallen into the fountain along with the book and there was no fixing that.

"I'll just have to rewrite it…" he said in a weak voice.

Hesitating, Ana chewed her lip. "When will you have time to do that if you're learning to play baseball?"

Disappointment roiled inside him, and he set the book down slowly on his night table. "I guess you're right."

She smiled, trying to smooth over the tension in the room. "Okay, so let's go home and get my stuff and we'll work on that. I'm sure you'll pick it up quickly."

"Sure." Woodenly, Tony left his own room, the notebook sitting crinkled and desolate in the darkness. Ana jostled his arm, and he followed her, though he wanted nothing but to go through the book and reclaim all the lost words.

They snuck out of the house without saying anything to his family. What did it matter? His whole world had been turned upside down and even if they wanted him to stay, he wasn't truly himself.

As he followed Ana, she talked nonstop. "You *do* at least understand the rules of baseball, right? Of course, you do…" But she launched into a detailed explanation anyway, pointing out how important a job the pitcher had. He stopped listening when she started talking about how to pitch because there was no point in hearing it when he knew he wouldn't be able to do it.

When she started talking about the new bat she'd just bought, he finally piped up just to say, "Ana. Shh."

"I—" She put a hand over her heart. "Did you just—"

"Yes. Shh."

"Why?"

"You won't let me work with my book so I'm rewriting in my head, okay?" He breathed out a long sigh. "And then, when I'm finished learning your silly game, I'll write it all out."

"Finished? You'll never be finished learning baseball. Are you kidding?" She stopped and turned to him. "I've been playing for, like, five years, T. You can't learn it as well as me *and* write in your head at the same time."

He crossed his arms and tilted his head. "Watch me."

"I—" She huffed when Tony started walking again. Catching up to him, she said, "I mean, I like your sense of determination, but come on."

"How hard can it be? It's just throwing a ball, right?"

She clenched her jaw and then forced herself to loosen up. "It's *not* just throwing a ball, but okay. How about I rewrite your book while you *throw a ball?*"

He gave her a sharp look. "Don't touch my book, Ana."

"How hard can it be?" she sassed. "It's just putting words on a page."

"Okay, I'll say it again. Don't. Touch. My. Book."

"*Fine.*"

Stomping ahead, she rounded the corner towards her street. A pang of longing hit her square in the chest. She wanted to go home but not like this. Tony dragged his feet behind her, and she was tempted to leave him behind. But she knew it would look weird to her family if "Tony" went into the house first. So, biting back a sigh, she slowed down for him, looped her arm through his, and half dragged him to her home.

"Ana…" He tugged on her elbow as they approached the house. "Do you have medicine in there?"

She gave him a sympathetic look and nodded. She knew her cramps could get bad and Tony wasn't used to that kind of pain. Normally she never took anything unless she was about to play a game. But she supposed she could spare one for Tony.

The old porch steps groaned as she went up the steps, despite her making a concerted effort to walk around the worst spots. Tony wasn't a big guy, but he was bigger than her and she guessed the stairs didn't like that. She wasn't a fan of it, either, but didn't have any choice. She helped herself to the front door and then ushered him inside.

In a whisper, she said, "Go say hi to Abuela. I'll grab you something from the cabinet."

Tony didn't ask which cabinet, what something, or even where Abuela was. Resigned to his fate, he simply made his way through the house, taking an educated guess that he would find her in the same spot as yesterday. Sure enough, there was the older woman sitting in a battered armchair in front of a TV that was currently turned off. She was snoring softly but as soon as Tony walked in, her eyes flew open.

"Hi, Abuela," he said softly.

She mumbled something he couldn't understand. But he did understand the arm waving gesture she made, and he came close enough for her to grab his hand. She pulled with more force than he thought she could muster until he'd nearly fallen into her lap. Turned out she wanted to kiss his cheek which he let her do before straightening.

Someone cleared their throat and Tony turned, relieved to see Ana standing in the doorway...even if she was still in his body. She smiled at Abuela and said, "Hi, Doña Anita."

Abuela's eyes narrowed, and she muttered, "*¿Quien es este chico?*"

"Oh, I'm just a friend," Ana said quickly, putting her hands up.

Now Abuela's eyebrows rose, and her gaze darted quickly to Tony and then back to Ana. "You are so pale. You speak Spanish?"

"Not well," Tony said, cutting off the conversation. Ana was about to dig them into a large grave if she carried on a conversation that he couldn't follow. "Anyway, we have a...project we're working on. So, we have to go. Right...Tony?"

"Yeah." Ana nodded but her gaze was still on Abuela. "It was nice to meet you."

Abuela merely huffed and reached out for the convertor to turn the TV on. Tony patted her shoulder for Ana's sake and then left, Ana trailing behind him. "So, what's the plan?" he asked when they were out of earshot.

Ana held out her hand. "Here, take this."

Tony picked up the pill that felt like it was at least half the size of a baseball. His eyes widened. "What is it?"

"Just take it," she said in an exasperated voice. She watched as he put it in his mouth and half-gagged trying to get it down. He could have found some water, but evidently chose not to. "I don't exactly have refills on those, so that'll have to last. You'll be fine by tomorrow anyway."

"Because I'll be in my own body?"

"I wish."

Ignoring the slight, Ana went to another door off the main entrance. It turned out that was the door to the garage and when Tony looked inside, he gasped. The entire thing was filled with sports stuff. Bikes, soccer balls and nets, a rack of hockey sticks and a goal, and baseball gloves, helmets, balls, and even bases. Ana suppressed an eyeroll and went over to "her" corner.

"Here's my stuff," she said. "Don't touch anything else. My brother and his friends keep all their junk here and so long as it stays away from my stuff, I don't complain."

"Why so many hockey sticks?" came out of his mouth while he was still taking it all in.

Ana just sighed as she picked up a ball and two gloves, and then looked around. "Just don't touch them. Where's my new bat?"

"In your bedroom." Tony couldn't help blushing as he said it. It was weird enough that he'd been in her bedroom. Sleeping in her bed in her body was even worse.

"Wait here."

Tony had no choice. He waited in the weird sports-filled garage, thinking about how his own garage at home held two cars and a few bikes. He and his sisters were never particularly sporty growing up. Maddy was the only one who came close—and she'd been a cheerleader and dancer. But seeing a box full of different types of balls was pretty enticing to him, even if he wasn't athletic.

Ana returned before curiosity got the better of him, brand-new bat in tow. "You ready?"

He wasn't, but he nodded and followed her back through the house to the backyard. She didn't stop there, and he only caught a glimpse of the gardens, which were overgrown with weeds, and an old porch glider that looked like it had seen better days. Heading all the way to the back, she scooted through a gap in the old chain-link fence, waving her hand impatiently for him to follow.

There was a field back there, with tall grass surrounding some metal transmission towers. Tony questioned the safety of playing in a spot like this, but Ana told him it was just fine and that she did it all the time. She handed him her own glove—which she hated to do—and the ball before walking some distance away.

Crouching down like a baseball catcher, she said, "Okay, let's see what you got, Cleaver."

"Oh." He looked at the ball, pulled his arm way back, and then launched it. It fell halfway between them. "That's…that's what I've got."

"¡Ay de mí!" She sat on the ground and flopped backwards, flinging an arm over her face. "Just let me die here."

"Ana…" He jogged towards her, chuckling a bit. The medicine had started to kick in and he felt like he could finally think clearly. "I'll try again. Come on, Dellagusta, get up. This field is probably full of ticks."

Se hopped up and looked around with unease. "Alright, go get the—" She cut herself off when he opened his glove to show her he'd already picked up the ball. "Okay… Okay do it again, but actually do it."

Tony nodded and lifted his hand, but she stopped him. "You're all wrong," she said. She took his elbows and turned him, then made sure his feet were square on the ground. "Don't pull back. Just be…just be normal. Like this." She took the ball and showed him how to throw it without actually tossing it. "Can you do that?"

"I can try."

He didn't sound confident, but Ana didn't have much choice. She walked away from him again, held her glove up, and said, "Aim for me this time, please."

"Alright."

Trying to emulate what she'd shown him, he lifted his arm and threw the ball. She had to lean to her left to catch it but as she did a smile lit her face.

"Okay, now we're getting somewhere."

# Chapter Thirteen

Val had no choice but to take Sam all the way to her house, at least to get her glasses. How ridiculous that he'd gone all day without being able to see. The entire way there, he pulled on her loose sweatshirt like he thought that was going to help the outfit.

"Stop pulling on my clothes like that," she said.

"Why? It's not like I can make them any looser." He pulled one more time, before shoving his hands into the kangaroo pockets. "By the way, why are you wearing *that*?"

She sighed. "I just wanted to be comfortable."

"And…no one noticed?"

"No, *everyone* noticed."

He snickered, but didn't say anything. If she wanted to look great in his body, that was her prerogative. She just shook her head and dropped the argument. It wasn't worth the effort.

When they got to Val's house, there were no cars in the driveway, and she knew her younger siblings wouldn't be home yet. Juliette was at a chess meet and Harrison had soccer practice. She didn't intend to still be here when they all got home. She didn't want them to get the wrong idea about her and Sam.

Although...the right idea wasn't much better. They wouldn't believe it if she said she'd switched bodies with a boy at school and now he had to live with them until...what, exactly? Surely, they didn't really expect her to send him to her debate competition.

After punching in the number on the lock outside and letting herself in, Shadow immediately barked twice. She could hear the clicking of his claws as he rushed towards them. No...not towards them. To *her*. She laughed as he nuzzled her legs and licked her hand.

"Aw, Shadow, I miss you, too," she said softly. "Let's go get you a treat."

He panted happily and followed her through the house to the kitchen as Sam watched in amazement. He'd never seen Val so...happy. After giving them a moment together, Sam reached out his hand and rubbed the scruff of Shadow's neck.

"I'm surprised he recognizes me," she said softly.

"Yeah, he was weird with me yesterday," he answered. "I bet he feels better now knowing you're okay."

She gave him a look and he just laughed.

"Well, you *are* okay. Things could be worse."

"Yeah. Sure."

"Come on, Val." In one swift motion, he hopped up on the counter, his legs splayed in a most unladylike fashion. "Why don't you tell me all about your debate thingy?"

She huffed and said, "Why don't you close your legs?"

"Oh."

She went into the pantry for the treats she knew Shadow liked. A couple of bone-shaped, high-protein snacks for her big boy would do the trick. "My debate *thingy* is an actual competition. I got stuck on the pro side of an incinerator debate. So. Good luck with that."

"You mean like those garbage incinerators?"

"Yeah," she said with exasperation.

"Why? What's wrong with that?"

"What's *wrong* with that?" Her mouth gaped open as she waited for Sam to take his question back. When he didn't, she asked, "Are you kidding?"

"No?"

"Honestly, Sam." She threw her hands in the air and Shadow's ears perked up, as if sensing her irritation. "It's bad enough we make so many toxins and waste. And you want to burn it all and send it up into the atmosphere? Destroy everything out there, too?"

Hunching his shoulders, he said, "I'm just saying that there are probably other hills to die on."

"Yeah, and they're all filled with trash. It's no wonder the aliens don't want to visit us."

"Wait…" Half of his mouth tilted up. "You believe in aliens?"

Val hesitated, wondering how she was supposed to backtrack from that. "Nah… I mean…" She rolled her eyes. "Not necessarily. I'm just saying if they *do* exist, there's a reason they haven't made first contact."

"Okay. Okay so you think the aliens are, what, more cultured than us or something?"

"Absolutely."

Laughter bubbled out of Sam. "That's the silliest thing I've ever heard. Are you serious right now?"

She bit her lip and looked away. "We're veering wildly off topic. Let me go get my cue card." She glanced at him. "*And* my glasses. Must be nice to have perfect vision all the time," she muttered as she walked away. Of course, she *had* been enjoying not having to wear glasses for the past few days but she wouldn't admit it out loud.

Sam rolled his eyes and then patted Shadow's head. In another life, he might have had a dog like this. He'd asked Ty once—he would never have dreamed of asking their dad—but Ty had said until they were in a "better position" they couldn't keep a dog. Sam got it. He needed to be able to pay for it himself if he wanted one. Maybe one day, then.

"Okay!" Val called out loudly as she re-entered the kitchen. "I get to have one cue card only at the debate so I put as much as I could on it. Here you go."

His eyebrows drew in as he took the proffered cue card. It was filled, margins and all, front and back, with the teeniest writing he'd ever seen. He tried to read the first line, but he could barely focus on it. "I can't read this."

"Try it with these," she said in a teasing voice. She held out a pair of plain black round-rimmed glasses.

He put them on, and he could indeed see the words better. But it didn't mean he could read it any better. "I...I still can't read this. I'm sorry."

He tried to hand it back to her, but she just stared at it and looked back up at him. "What do you mean? That's my nicest writing."

"I mean my dyslexia clearly followed me to this body." He let out an irritated breath. "This is too small and cramped for me to...sort through."

"Oh." Val didn't even know Sam had dyslexia. "I'm...I'm only allowed one cue card."

He scratched the back of his neck. "Well...can you rewrite it bigger, and I'll just memorize it?"

"Memorize it?" she asked in a shocked voice.

He chuckled. "I have *dyslexia*. Not short-term memory loss. I could probably memorize it."

"I...I guess that could work." She dropped her hand. She'd worked *so* hard on making the perfect cue card. Now she wouldn't even get to use it, and neither would Sam. What else could possibly go wrong? "What about you? What should I do for you?"

"Just do whatever the photographer tells you to do," he answered nonchalantly.

"Are you joking?" She watched him casually get up, get himself a glass, and pour some water into it from the tap of all places. "Sam. I mean that. Are you serious?"

"Yup." He downed the water in one go.

"What else am I supposed to do?" She lifted a hand and Shadow nudged it, prompting her to rub his head and back. "I have to do something before then. I can't just...hang out with your brother until Saturday."

"Why not?"

"Because..." She threw her hands up. How was she supposed to explain she didn't even want to hang out with her own brother most of the time, let alone Sam's? "I don't know what to do with him."

Sam's face scrunched up. "What do you mean?"

"I mean like he's broody and quiet and then *asks about your life* and I don't know anything about your life. So what do I do with that?"

He bit his lip instead of telling her that maybe if *she* asked about him, then she'd know the answers. "He's not a monster, Val. All you have to do is exist alongside him. And then do what the photographer says."

"What does that even mean?" she asked, her voice rising a notch. It was still a good octave lower than hers and it felt weird to her.

"You said you'd go do my photoshoot, right?"

"Yeah."

"Well...the photographer tells you what to do. It'll feel weird, but just listen closely and do whatever they say. Don't worry, it's like the easiest thing in the world." He flicked a hand in the air as if dismissing his own role in the whole thing.

"Couldn't you just...reschedule it?"

Instead of scoffing at her like he wanted to, he said, "Couldn't you reschedule your debate competition?"

"*No.*" She shook her head and Shadow nudged her with his nose, this time straight into her abdomen. "I don't just get to choose when competitions happen."

"Right." He looked at her for a moment, wishing she wasn't carrying around his money-making face. Although, when he thought about it, that frown she had on was kind of perfect for an angsty pose, but that was about the only good thing he could say about it. "Now that we both know how schedules work, can we get on with our—I mean, each other's lives?"

Dropping her gaze, she sighed. "I just don't know how to live with your brother. It feels weird."

He tried not to take it personally. After all, it was a little weird to only live with his brother and not either of his parents. But instead of comforting her, he said, "What about your family, Val? What am I supposed to do with them? I can't cook and I don't know them."

Irritation rose up inside her. "Can't you just fake it?"

He crossed his arms. "No, I can't. I don't know what it's like to live with a nice, happy family that enjoys spending time together. Okay?"

Val paused to process his words. "Sam..." she said softly.

Wrapping his arms around himself, he looked away. "Forget I said that. I'll just...figure it out."

She touched his arm lightly, but he didn't respond. "It's not hard to be with them," she assured him. "They just look out for each other and that's all you have to do. Kind of like you do with Tony."

Warmth spread through Sam's chest that Val had pegged their friendship correctly. But still, he said, "Tony does most of the looking out. I'm just...there."

She resisted the urge to roll her eyes. "You don't...pick a fight with people who make fun of him, or shield him from hurtful criticisms, or give him as much of your spare time as you possibly can? It's all one-sided?"

"Yes," he lied.

"Okay, well, sounds like an easy job for me. If all I have to do is look pretty and stand next to him…" She shrugged, hoping he'd call her bluff.

Instead, he turned back to her, daggers shooting from his eyes. "How many times are you going to remind me that all I'm good for is looking good?"

"What?" She put her hands up. "That's not—"

"You've said it enough!" He shook his head. "Don't you think I know that? Why else do you think I've been trying so hard to get a modeling gig. You know, you, and Tony, and Ana… You all can do whatever you want with your lives and go far with that. But me? *This*—" he gestured to her borrowed face "—is all I have. So, please don't mess that up for me."

She swallowed hard. She'd clearly hit a nerve with her lighthearted teasing. "Okay," she whispered. "I'll do whatever the photographer says. Wait! It's not a…" she lowered her voice to a whisper "…*nude* photoshoot, is it?"

He closed his eyes and said, "Valerie…" under his breath. Choosing not to even answer, he said, "Look, you don't have to hang out with Ana if you don't want to. Like, I won't make you. But our families will find it really weird if you don't. You don't have to be best friends, but…"

"It's fine," she said quietly. "I don't have any friends at school, so at least you get off easy there." Sam opened his mouth to answer her but she didn't want to let him. "I usually take Shadow out every day after school. Don't forget to scoop. See you later, Sam."

"Are you leaving already?"

She could hear in his voice an uncertainty. She briefly wished he wanted her to stay just to have her around. But she knew it was really his body he wanted to keep close by. "I'll go and rewrite my notes for you. We can meet again later. Or tomorrow at school."

She started to walk away, and Shadow immediately rose and followed her. She tried to tell him to stay but it was as if he sensed she was leaving. Sam smiled as Shadow eagerly trailed her to the door.

"You're not even going to stay long enough to take him out?" he asked.

"No. Shadow, no. I'm sorry. Sam will take you out, okay?" She scratched the scruff of his neck and then kissed the top of his head. "I'm sorry, buddy." She met Sam's gaze. "I'm sorry to you, too. I'm not very photogenic."

"It's okay," he said, as he opened the front door for her. "*I* am."

# Chapter Fourteen

Val waited until she was a good two blocks away before letting her tears fall. How was she supposed to get Sam to give a convincing argument when he couldn't even read her cue card? She supposed it helped that he at least agreed with the side she'd been given, but on the other hand that made things worse. How could she work with someone who wanted to burn all the toxins in the world?

Swiping her tears away, she gathered her resolve. Sam could believe the Earth was flat for all she cared. It didn't make a difference. The only thing that mattered was getting through this weekend. And then they could sort out the rest of their lives later.

Dejectedly, she brought herself back to Sam's apartment. She was surprised to see Ty in there, sitting at the table with some textbooks in front of him. He glanced at her briefly, his eyebrows raised in a silent greeting, and then looked back down.

"Sorry I'm so late," Val felt compelled to say.

Frowning, he tapped on his phone. "It's like 4:30, dude."

"You weren't expecting me right after school?"

His frown deepening, he said, "You know I don't care how late you are as long as I know where you're sleeping. I'm trying to concentrate, Sam."

"Sorry," Val mumbled.

With no other option, she went to Sam's room. She knew she could never make this place her home. Not when it was like this. Why wouldn't he have his bed by the window and his dresser next to the closet so he could get dressed more efficiently? And then there would be space for the full-length mirror next to the dresser. It made so much more sense.

Pushing away her uneasiness and ignoring the many boundaries she was crossing, Val began the tedious process of rearranging Sam's room. It meant she had to pick up all the stray clothes, left-behind dishes, and one mouldy sandwich forgotten under the bed. And she had to poke around the kitchen for a broom, because she couldn't very well move furniture without sweeping underneath it.

Once she'd moved the bed underneath the window, she then pushed his dresser across the floor with surprising ease. Under all these gaudy clothes were a set of muscles she might have previously ignored. They did, however, make it much easier to accomplish her unnecessary task. She even used those muscles to wash all the bedding. If she had to stay here in this body, she might as well sleep in a clean bed.

Ty never once acknowledged her as she went back and forth between the kitchen and Sam's room for various cleaning supplies. He'd even put on headphones by the time she went in search of laundry machines, which were thankfully in an alcove next to the bathroom.

With nothing now to do but wait for the laundry, Val sprawled out on the bare bed, hands behind her head. If she were at home, she would have been in the living room with the rest of her family, probably reading a book. She looked around the room. There wasn't a single book in sight. Not big readers, these guys.

But could she blame Sam? With a condition like dyslexia, it was probably hard to dive into a book and really enjoy it. And now he thought he'd be able to *memorize* her entire debate speech, point for point. What a disaster that would be!

She took the cue card out of her pocket and glared down at it. What a useless little piece of paper. With a sigh, she put it on the desk and opened up Sam's laptop. Surely he wouldn't mind if she used it to rewrite the card in an appropriate—and larger—font.

As soon as the screen turned on, Val caught sight of the most beautiful digital rendering of a human-like creature. She recognized him—it was the man from the drawings. She had stacked all those papers neatly on his desk before moving the whole thing and now she scrabbled to find the one she'd seen earlier.

After finding it, she held the paper up to the screen. Yup, that was the one. The character with the horns, green skin, and large teeth. The digital version was much more cleaned up and vibrant, though she liked both. She had to wonder, though—why had Sam copied this picture instead of making up his own?

Shaking her head, she put the picture back down. Turning back to the laptop, she almost clicked on the word processor, but her eye was drawn to a folder called "Art." She clicked on that instead and found the whole thing full of pictures similar to the desktop background. Some of them featured the same character, but then there were others, too.

She couldn't help scrolling through them. Along with the greenish ogre dude was a softer, more feminine character. Same protruding type of teeth, but her lips were fuller, her shiny black hair longer, and her skin a more emerald shade of green. The ogres had a friend, too—a pink-toned girl with crisp white wings. She had full armour on, which covered her body but didn't conceal her shapely form, and she carried a bow and arrows.

Val gasped when she saw in the corner of the picture of the three of them a signature which could only be Sam's. It had a very defined S and D and some squiggles. But…but that meant… All these pictures were *his*? How could he hide such a brilliant talent from, well, everyone? Why weren't these plastered all over the place instead of his headshots?

Having totally lost sight of her goal, she clicked through more pictures. Some of them were settings—landscapes featuring a crumbling old castle, or a dock with mystical-looking sailboats. All of them were the same art style, though several weren't signed. Val didn't need the signature anyway. She knew the truth, though she still couldn't figure out why.

"Oh, Sam," she whispered. "Who knew you had this in you?"

*     *     *

Tony got tired of practicing pitching far too early for Ana's liking. His arm hurt—or so he said. Though when she finally relented and said they could take a break, he promptly sat on the ground and wrapped his arms around his midriff.

"I thought the medicine helped," she said in a disappointed voice.

"It did. A little." He gave her a miserable look and curled even more into himself. "How do you live like this?"

Suppressing an eyeroll, Ana picked up the baseball glove he'd unceremoniously dropped on the ground. "You'll probably be fine tomorrow."

"*Probably*?"

"Yeah, probably."

"Ugh." Letting go of his waist, he lay back in the grass he'd claimed was likely crawling with ticks. "I just want to go home, Ana."

"You can't go home."

"Why not?" he said in an irritable voice.

"Well…" She stood over him, a quirky little grin on her handsome face.

"You can't go to *your* home. But I guess you could go to mine."

"Thanks…"

With a groan he rose and dusted off his backside. Ana pursed her lips when he seemed to be taking an awfully long time with his task. "Would you stop?" she finally said.

He dropped his hand and looked at her, his cheeks tingeing pink. "Sorry. I was checking for ticks."

"Uh huh. Go home, T."

She shoved the gloves and bat at him and whirled around. What was she supposed to do without him? She didn't want to go back to his place with his sisters and his ruined notebook and his…*boy clothes*. But a glance over her shoulder confirmed he was doing exactly what she said.

She nearly tripped and when she looked down, there was her old, battered baseball. She picked it up and called out, "Tony!"

When he turned, she lobbed the ball at him. He caught the ball easily and held it up to show her. "Nice catch!" she called out.

He smiled. "Thanks!"

Ana's heart dropped when he turned around and kept going like he didn't need her. They were in this together, but it seemed he couldn't handle being her. Or maybe he really couldn't handle the pain.

Regardless, she had no choice but to go back to his house, hoping that his family wouldn't pester her too much. She had a lot on her plate and she didn't want to deal with them. But when she got there, and saw the sad state of Tony's precious journal, she felt even worse.

Not knowing who to turn to, she got out Tony's phone and…texted Val. Begging for her help. Val's response was quick: "Sure. Not like I'm doing anything but sitting here being cute."

Ana smiled. Sam *was* pretty attractive, but she could tell Val didn't care at all about that. And being in the body of an attractive person wasn't nearly as enticing as the idea seemed. Ana knew that now.

It didn't take long for Val to get to Tony's house and when she did, they immediately locked themselves in Tony's room away from his sisters' prying ears and eyes.

"Alright, let's see the book," Val said. Ana handed it to her, and Val frowned at the crinkled mess. "Ana...what happened? How'd you do so much damage to this?"

"Well..." Ana shuffled her feet, chewing on her bottom lip. "I just got a new bat. You know, from the sports store? And I was, like, showing off my moves. With my bat? Because I look pretty good with a bat, right?"

Val blinked at her. "I wouldn't know. I've never seen you play."

"Okay. I do look good, though. I'm a pretty good player. But I accidentally hit his book and knocked it into the fountain."

"Uh huh. And who were you trying to impress?"

"No one." But even as she said it, she could feel her cheeks heat up. Curse Tony's fair complexion.

A small smile grew on Val's face. "Were you trying to impress *Tony*?"

"No...no..." Ana's face went even redder. She wasn't normally a blusher, but she didn't have much choice in this body. "I was just, like, near him. While I did my super cool baseball moves."

"Ana..." Val's smile stretched across her face. "Do you...*like* Tony?"

"N-no," Ana stammered. "Well, not like... I don't...not...not...like him."

Val stopped for a moment think about the meaning. But it didn't matter. Ana's reaction spoke loud enough. "So...is it the poetry that got you hooked or those adorable blue eyes?"

Putting her head in her hands, Ana groaned and sat on the bed. "It's just... He's so sweet and soft and I don't know why I like that because he's different than any other guy I've ever met. Do you know what I mean?"

Val didn't have any special affinity for any of the guys she knew. But she could appreciate that Tony was different. It surprised her that Ana felt that way for him, but she wasn't here to judge. "Yeah. I know what you mean. He's a big softie and you're a big softie."

Lifting her head out of her hands, Ana gave Val a pathetic look. "Okay, yes, I like him. I'm into him and now I'm literally…" She stopped and sighed before finishing with, "in him."

"Well…" Val sat next to Ana, biting back a chuckle. "Why don't you show me the book and we'll figure out how to get Tony to fall in love with you?"

Ana groaned again and gestured at her borrowed body. "Like this? Good luck with that." But she wasn't going to argue anymore, not if Val would seriously help her with the book.

Val finally opened the book and drew in a sharp breath. "I mean…the ink didn't run too much but his writing is barely legible. I think we should just try to type this out as best as possible."

"You mean…read his book?" Ana said tentatively.

Val stared at her as if she had two heads. How did Ana expect to fix this without reading any part of it? "Yeah. We have to read the book."

Ana sighed. "Okay."

But Ana just sat there and Val, having too much sympathy in her heart, handed her the book. "Here. Why don't you read it out loud and I'll type it up? We could probably get this done quickly."

"You'd really do that with me?"

Ignoring the hope in Ana's voice, Val rose and went to the desk where Tony's laptop was sitting. "Again—" she opened the laptop and sat down "—I wasn't doing anything but looking pretty."

"You kind of like Sam, don't you?" Ana said with a teasing voice.

"No," Val said flatly. "You just have as fanciful an imagination as Tony. Read."

Ana nodded and finally focused on the words in the book. "'The sun hung low in the sky, casting a hazy…brown…' I think? 'Brown glow over the…' I don't know. 'Mountain.' We'll pretend it says that. 'Valentino—'" Ana stopped abruptly and frowned. "'*Valentino* licked his…tusks?' Seriously? What is happening?"

Val turned quickly and held her hand out. "Let me see that." After Ana handed her the book, Val's eyes trailed along the words. "'Valentino licked his *tusks*, a smile curving his sea green lips.' Oh my *gosh*!"

"What?" Ana asked in a startled voice.

"This guy is an orc."

"Not…a Latino?"

"No, no. He's a fantasy character with green skin and funky teeth. And Sam's been drawing him!"

"Okay…" Ana's eyebrows drew together. "But he's a fantasy *Latino* character, right? You can't just use a name like Valentino and not be Latino."

Val laughed out loud. "He has tusks and green skin and look— He's about to talk to a centaur!"

Ana lifted an eyebrow. "A black centaur?"

Val looked over the words. There was nothing about that in the book. "Maybe… We'll just add it in. Tony will thank us later."

Val returned the book to Ana and turned back to the laptop. Before she continued reading, Ana asked, "Are the drawings any good?"

"They're amazing," Val said plainly. "Read."

# Chapter Fifteen

When Tony got back to Ana's place, a strange scent tickled his nose. It was good, in a sweet way, but also somehow bad, like there were too many conflicting palates. Ana's name was called several times before Tony realized *he* was the one who was supposed to respond. It was Abuela's voice, and she sounded like she was in a good mood.

"Hey, Abuela," he said as he entered the kitchen.

She was hunched over the stove, steam wafting around her face. But her posture and the heat didn't seem to bother her at all. In fact, she turned to him with a wide smile, extending a dish towards him. "*Enchiladas. ¡Come!*"

"Oh!" He took the dish, which held a rolled-up tortilla drizzled in a red sauce. "*Gracias.*"

Abuela mumbled something else while gesturing towards the dining room. She turned and started vigorously stirring whatever was in her pot, the wooden spoon clanking dully against the metal. Tony went to the dining room table and sat down. He was just about to dig into his enchilada when Ana's brother walked by. He pulled the fork out of Tony's hand and shook his head.

"Don't eat that."

Tony scowled at him. He'd barely eaten anything all day and he wasn't about to abstain over some ridiculous standard Ana's brother had for her. "Why not?"

Her brother's eyebrows scrunched up in confusion. "You know she can't cook anymore. I think the only seasoning she used was cinnamon. And that's not tomato sauce, it's pure hot sauce."

His frown deepening in disgust, Tony pushed the plate away. That explained the strange smells. "Then what am I supposed to eat?"

Her brother shrugged, which inexplicably brought tears to Tony's eyes. He blinked rapidly while the brother's frown softened. "Oh...oh no," her brother said. "Is it—" he lowered his voice "—your special time?"

Fighting the urge to roll his eyes, Tony said, "Yeah, man. It's my special time."

Her brother patted him on the shoulder. "I'll make you something, okay? But I gotta wait till Abuela's gone, 'cause you know what she's like."

"Oh...okay, sure. Thanks!"

Her brother tilted his head, his eyebrows scrunching together in concern. "Are you feeling okay today, *hermanita*?"

Tony nodded and tried to smile. He was most certainly not feeling okay in the slightest. But he couldn't tell Ana's brother that. "I'm fine," he whispered.

The brother nodded. "Okay. I'll make you some food."

As soon as he walked off, Tony texted Ana.

**Tony: What is your brother's name and is he serious about not eating Abuela's food?**

**Ana: Davide. Don't eat her food!!!**

Tony sighed. He was never going to make it to Ana's baseball game like this. He'd all but determined it was impossible to be Ana and he respected her for all she did. Maybe if he thought that enough times, he would magically appear back in his own body. Unfortunately, nothing happened, no matter how many good thoughts he had about her.

A few minutes later, Davide came back holding a plate with a single burrito on it. Tony would take it.

"Thanks," he said as he immediately picked it up.

"Don't worry," Davide said in a surprisingly soft voice. "*Mami* will be home soon, and she'll take care of you."

Tony swallowed hard. He'd rather be at home with his own mother and father. He'd even take his sisters' overbearing doting at this point, but it was kind of Davide to give Ana a little attention. "Thanks."

Tony wondered how Sam was and if he was faring any better. But Sam was the type to always say he was fine. And if Tony complained too much, Sam might barge over here and then make things even stranger than they already were.

Sam was anything but fine, of course. From the moment he'd stepped into Val's home, he'd been accosted by Harrison, Juliette, Mr. Davis, *and* the dog. They'd complained at him about everything from coming home "too late" to not being there when he was supposed to help the family.

But at the same time, he caught Harrison and Juliette laughing and teasing each other, and after a while, it occurred to him he was supposed to be in on the jokes, too. Maybe it was the humour that Val was used to, but Sam wasn't. He and Ty didn't tease each other. Sure, they could laugh over a good joke or two. But not at each others' expenses.

When Harrison playfully insulted Juliette's hairdo and Juliette jokingly told Harrison it matched the C he'd gotten on his last math test, Sam had cringed, fearing the worst. Mr. Davis was *right there* hearing the entire conversation while they verbally jousted back and forth. But Mr. Davis had laughed it off before telling his son to study harder next time and telling

Juliette she looked beautiful today.

Mr. Davis did turn his smile towards Sam and complimented him, too. He even sounded more genuine than when he'd spoken to Juliette. Sam just nodded and ran moist palms down the sides of his pants. He'd never had a parent tell him he was beautiful or handsome, or anything that felt warm and fuzzy.

Ty did an okay job filling the spaces their parents had left in Sam's life. But it wasn't like the way Mr. Davis gave him a side hug before reminding him Val had apparently offered to go read to the old folks tomorrow night.

What a joy that would be for Sam.

*      *      *

All four spent a restless night. Ana had given up transcribing Tony's book after sifting through his handwriting had gotten too tiring. Val had had to leave anyway since she still needed to rewrite her debate argument for Sam. And Sam, after all the weird nonsense Val's family put him through, was eager to go to bed, but could barely sleep.

Tony was the only one who felt remotely refreshed in the morning due to Ana's period pains finally abating, it seemed. Or maybe he was getting used to them. And he didn't want to get used to being in her body.

As soon as they met up at school, they immediately told each other, "We have to fix this!"

Of course, it was what they'd been trying to do since the blackout, and the solution still hadn't come. At least, not easily.

They barely saw each other all day, despite Sam and Tony wanting to stay close and Ana and Val trying to act like best friends. Val was pulled into the school counselor's office for a meeting to discuss her—or rather *Sam's* future—during which Val had sat politely, nodded, and answered all questions as blankly as possible. The counselor hadn't been impressed with her "attitude" and scheduled another meeting for next week, which Val hoped she wouldn't have to attend as well.

And while Ana was frantically searching for Val, Arthur stopped her to pick her brain. Well, not hers. *Tony's*. Arthur was working on his next roleplaying campaign and Tony had been *so* helpful to him last time. Extricating herself from that conversation hadn't been easy. She wasn't creative, at least not like Tony, and didn't know anything about roleplaying games.

Tony was stuck having to spend time with the other female athletes, which might have been nice were he in his own body. But he sensed something subtle in the way the other girls interacted with him. They seemed to only tolerate his presence, rather than enjoy it like good friends would. And at first, he wondered if they *knew*. But then it occurred to them that they were probably always like this with Ana, which made him a little sad. She wasn't that bad!

Sam had it worse, though. *No one* even attempted to hang out with him. No one called Val's name, asked to partner with Sam in groups in class, or sat with him at lunch. Even Tony didn't, but that was because all the field hockey and lacrosse players had gathered around his table, and he'd been stuck. Sam wasn't used to the quiet or having no friends.

Eventually, feeling sorry for the girls and for themselves, Sam and Tony had naturally gravitated back towards each other. While Sam lamented that he had to go read to the old people, Tony groaned about Ana's baseball practice.

"Oh come on," Sam whispered as they sat in the library together. "That's way better than having to...to *read*."

Tony stared at him for a moment. "Have you...met me? Reading is my whole personality."

Sam cracked a grin. "Wouldn't it be great if you and I could switch bodies right now? I'd play Ana's game in a heartbeat."

"And I would be thrilled to read whatever whenever for Val."

"Alright, so let's try it, then!"

"Shhh." Tony looked around them, but no one else had seemed to notice or care about Sam's outburst. "Sam, honestly, if I could make a body switch happen, I'd do that with my own body."

"Oh. Right."

Tony smiled sympathetically. "You'll be fine tonight. All you have to do is read everything one syllable at a time. Take it slow and do your best. Right?"

"I guess..."

"The good thing is—" Tony's smile brightened "—since they're old you can read slowly and loudly and they won't care. Oh, but do remember Val's glasses."

Sam chuckled and readjusted the glasses he'd put on that morning. Everything was a little clearer with them on, but the frames were so bland. It was like Val purposefully tried as hard as possible to look hideous. And she had to try hard since she was naturally gorgeous, but Sam wouldn't be the one to tell her.

"And all you have to do is...throw a ball." Sam clasped Tony on the shoulder. "Easy peasy, right? But don't throw her shoulder out, she'll never forgive you."

"*Ugh.*"

*　　*　　*

It was all fun and games...until Tony had to actually play the game. He couldn't decide whether it was better or worse that Ana had come out to watch the team practice. He felt like he stuck out like a sore thumb as he made his way out to the field with the other girls. Looking around for an open spot, he waited, wondering what to do now.

When he glanced at Ana for some silent help, she rolled her eyes and made a motion like she was throwing something. Right. He was the pitcher. Letting out a long, anxious breath, he made his way to the pitcher's mound.

"Alright, ladies!" Coach Anderson clapped her hands together. "Show me what you got today!"

Tony didn't have a whole lot, but to be fair, he wasn't one of the ladies. For Ana's sake though—she was so tense she looked like she would crack all his bones just by sitting on the bleachers—he would try his hardest.

However, he forgot Sam's advice and nearly destroyed Ana's shoulder making his first pitch. It went too fast and too far and wasn't anywhere close to his target. The catcher—Tony couldn't see who it was since she already had her helmet on—looked over at the stray ball that was rolling towards the back fence. Slowly, she rose up from her crouched position, grabbed the ball, and lobbed it back to Tony. At least he caught it since she hadn't thrown it hard.

"Want to try that again, Dellagusta?" Anderson called out.

He didn't, but he would. He glanced at Ana quickly. She still had that distressed look on her face, the kind he used to make when he had to watch Sam suffer through reading aloud in class. And what had he always told Sam?

"Take it slow, do your best."

Tony took a deep breath, ball in hand, and got in position for a real pitch. He remembered not to pull his arm too far back like Ana had shown him. He tossed the ball, and it was kind of a slow pitch, but it was right on its mark. And because it was so slow, the batter swung too early and hit the ball at the wrong angle, causing it to fly up and out of bounds.

That was…better. One quick look at Ana, and it seemed she'd relaxed the tiniest little bit. She nodded at him, and he threw his next pitch a little harder but still under his control. He could do this. He could totally not screw up in front of Ana inside her body. Everything was fine.

# Chapter Sixteen

Ana didn't stick around to watch the end of practice. She cringed at how bad Tony had made her look and she knew if she stayed any longer, she'd get right on that field and yell at him. And she didn't want to yell at him. Their predicament was bad enough without her making him feel worse.

So, she went back "home" to try to transcribe more of Tony's book. She'd quickly learned that it wasn't a complete story—it was snippets and scenes and half a plot with characters that did things Ana didn't understand. At least Tony clearly marked where a new scene started, usually adding in a short description of where it should go in the book.

But that left her trying to piece together a story without all the information. She'd just been introduced to a new character, a fairy who'd left her quaint small-town life of magic behind to enter the military. Everyone made fun of her because "fairies don't fight." And also, because her name was Sparkle. Ana found herself inexplicably drawn to her.

And as she read more, she found that Valentino also felt himself drawing closer to Sparkle, but in a very different way. Tony had a little romance going on in his book and *now* it was getting interesting. Ana had to admit though, the battle scenes were pretty good on their own. But she wished she knew how to piece together all these little bits.

Ana's eyes roved over the next scene in which she was pretty sure Valentino was going to try to kiss the bloodthirsty little fairy. Would she let him?

A knock on the door startled her so much she tossed the book in the air. She looked up as Maddy entered the room. Ana deserved that for keeping the door open, she supposed. Putting a hand over her heart, she leaned down to pick up the book.

"You scared me," Ana said.

"Aw, sorry," Maddy said as she sat on Tony's bed. "I just came to check on you. You've been so quiet lately."

"I'm fine," Ana said tersely. "I've been...trying to type up this stuff."

"Oh! Finally! Good for you. I can't wait to read the finished product." Maddy bobbed her eyebrows, but Ana just grunted. "What...you have nothing to say to that? You might actually let me read it one day?"

"Yeah... In fact, you can read it now and help me figure out my own awful handwriting." Ana shoved the book at Maddy.

"Oh-oh!" Maddy caught the book and carefully opened up the first crinkled page. "Are you sure?"

"*Yes.*" Hastily, Ana opened Tony's laptop before she changed her mind. "I can't figure out how all the stuff goes together."

"Stuff...goes together?"

"Yeah. There's battle scenes, and he's about to kiss a fairy, and also I think he has daddy issues, but we haven't actually seen the daddy yet. And I don't know how it all *goes* together."

"Oh." Maddy frowned. "Tony...are you feeling okay?"

"No. No, I'm not." Ana let out a frustrated sigh. "I'm not, like, a book person, okay? I don't know how writers write full books. I'm not—"

Maddy lifted an eyebrow. "Not what?"

"*Tony!*"

"*Oh.*"

"Yeah. So can you please help me fix this?"

Maddy's eyes narrowed, and Ana swallowed hard. She couldn't believe she'd just blurted that out to Tony's sister. Maybe she could backtrack now, take it all back.

But then Maddy said, "If you're not Tony, who are you and why are you reading his book?"

"My name's Ana." Nope. No going back now. "And I'm the one who got the book wet, alright?"

Maddy gasped and pulled the book close to herself. "You got it wet *and* you're reading it? I'm sorry, I can't let you do that. Especially when he's not even here to know about it."

"I'm trying to help him!"

"How? You said yourself you're not a book person."

"Yeah, but—" Ana stopped and stared at Maddy. "Wait…you actually believe me?"

Shifting on the bed, Maddy dropped her gaze. "Strange things happen in this town, you know."

"Okay…" Ana drawled. "Are you gonna help me or not?"

"No." Maddy's eyebrows drew in closely. "This is his special book. You shouldn't be reading this, and you never should have touched it."

"Don't you think I know that?" Ana reached out lightning fast and snapped the book away from Maddy.

"Hey!" Maddy knocked it out of Ana's hands and then they both reached for it at the same time.

When Maddy nearly took Ana out with her long fake nails, Ana shouted, "Enough! This is how I got into this mess in the first place!"

Maddy immediately pulled back and then, for some silly reason, started to laugh. "Oh…oh, that's good. That's hilarious."

"Stop that." Ana gingerly picked the book up. "I mean it, stop. Look, Tony's working really hard at…" She sighed. "At pitching for me, so either help me with this book or leave."

Maddy put her hands up and barely suppressed an eyeroll. "Alright, little miss Annie. I'll help you. He won't be happy when he finds out we read this, but I can see you're desperate."

"Thank you," Ana said graciously. But she couldn't help adding, "Also it's An*a*."

"Sorry," Maddy mumbled as she sat on the bed. "Alright, let's do this."

Ana smiled gratefully and passed the book to her. "I won't tell him you looked."

"It's fine…" Maddy carefully cracked the book open. "Okay, catch me up. What's happening? Is Valentino even still alive?"

"Still alive?" Huffing, Ana turned to Tony's laptop. "He's the main character. He can't die."

"Hmm…"

"Tony wouldn't do that."

"Oh, he would."

Ana chewed on her lip. Despite her initial reluctance to have anything to do with Tony's book, she'd gotten kind of…attached to his characters. She couldn't imagine killing off the hero. "He…he can't. I'm Tony and I'm deciding. Valentino lives."

"Okay." Maddy chuckled and tried to find the right spot.

Ana flipped a few pages for her and then pointed to where she'd stopped. "I think Valentino and Sparkle are about to kiss."

"There's no way," Maddy said. "Tony said there was no romance."

"Well, Tony's been lying about a lot of things lately." Ana bobbed her eyebrows. "Go ahead and read and I'll type."

Maddy cleared her throat. "'Sparkle's cheeks flushed a deep...*crimson* as Valentino tightened his hold on her neck. She flicked the blade of her switch, tempted to run it right through his...' I think that says 'heart.' I *think*. We'll go with that. And then... 'He loosened his grip enough for her to take in a surprised gasp just before—' Oh, *my*."

"What?" Ana said, her fingers stilling over the keyboard.

"Yup, you were right. He kisses her."

"Typical. Does she slap him?"

"Hmmm...no. But I could misread it for you if you like?"

"*Please*."

Maddy laughed out loud. "I like you, Ana. It's too bad you won't be sticking around."

Ana's eyebrows scrunched together. "What do you mean?"

Maddy shrugged. "You won't be in that body forever."

"How could you possibly know that?"

"Trust me. Just keep doing what you're doing and make sure he shows up at your game and...everything will be okay."

Ana looked away, her gaze focusing on the book. She didn't think Tony would be particularly impressed that she was going through his whole book to try to help him. And she still didn't know what she was supposed to do at his live reading. But Maddy sounded *so* confident. She had to try.

"Thanks, Maddy," she said genuinely. "I hope you're right."

"Oh, I am." Maddy flipped a page in Tony's book. "Anyway, after the kiss and no slap—"

"We're adding a slap."

Maddy smiled. "After the kiss and the slap, they both drop their weapons and decide to work together. Nice. I really can't wait to read this when it's published."

"Me, neither."

*      *      *

Val quickly finished typing up her debate speech. She couldn't believe the cue card filled up an entire two pages typed in a special font at a larger than normal size. She truly hoped it would help Sam, but that was a guess at best. Now all she had to do was print it and give it to him.

She went back out into the living room, which was empty. The sound of running water drew her to the kitchen. "Ty."

Sam's older brother shot her a glare over his shoulder before quickly turning back to the sink which she realized was full of soapy water and probably dirty dishes.

Ignoring that, she said, "Where's the printer?"

He scoffed into the sudsy sink. "At the library where you last used it."

"Oh. Okay, I'll be right back."

"Hey!" Ty called as she attempted to escape his bad mood. "Did you forget you make half the mess around here? You haven't done dishes in days."

"Uh, I... Um..." Val looked at the large clock on the wall next to Ty. The library will be closing soon. "I'll help when I get back, okay? It's important."

"Yeah, so are clean dishes," he muttered as she hastened away.

Val went back to Sam's laptop so she could email herself the document she'd made. She did feel a twinge of guilt as she left the apartment. She had no idea how many of Sam's chores she'd been neglecting, but who could focus on cleaning when her debate team needed her? Ty would just have to wait.

With Sam's long and sturdy legs, she rushed to the library and made it there with plenty of time to print her document. She smiled at the bespectacled librarian behind the desk who smiled back at her, but without the familiarity Val was used to. Right, because she didn't look like herself.

She looked like a boy who probably rarely came into the library.

As quickly as she could, Val printed her document from one of the public computer stations, paid with some change from Sam's wallet—she could pay him back—and left almost as quickly as she'd come. Normally she could spend hours at the library, browsing books, reading in their comfy chairs, or doing research.

As she left, she folded up her paper and tucked it into her back pocket. The front pocket was no good—the pants were too tight. All of Sam's pants were except for the grey sweatpants and she'd learned now not to wear those.

She took the fastest route home from the library. It went through a couple of back alleys that Val knew she never needed to worry about it, and cut across a train crossing where there was no road, only a walking path. Sam's feet may have never before seen these paths, but Val knew them by heart. She could have walked to and from the library blindfolded. One more shortcut over a bike path bridge and she'd arrived at her own backyard.

It wasn't fenced since it backed onto open brush that led to the river. No one ever came up to the back of their home because it was out of the way, but Val had many times begged her parents to put up a fence for Shadow's sake. He was a good boy, but the squirrels, bunnies, and even foxes that paid them a visit were far too great a temptation for him. They could never just let him roam outside by himself without being leashed up and it was a shame. Her parents had turned her down, though, even after the impressive slideshow presentation she'd made.

And in fact, she could hear Shadow barking even now through the large back bay window. It hadn't occurred to her before that he would sense her coming and now she could see two younger faces pressed up against the window. Harrison and Juliette. How was she supposed to explain her appearance to them like this?

Quickly, she scooted around the side of the house to the front and rang the doorbell. She should have expected Harrison and Juliette, but she still gave them an exasperated huff when she asked for…herself.

"Are you Val's boyfriend?" Harrison asked, his eyes narrowed to little slits.

Juliette's eyes were wide open however, innocent interest shining in them. "*Are* you?"

"*No.*" Val rolled her eyes and crossed her arms over her chest. "Can you please either let me in or go get Val?"

Harrison gave her one more glare before turning away. But Juliette leaned in the doorway and smiled at her. "If you're not her boyfriend, why are you here?"

"We're working on a school project." It was mostly the truth.

"Val doesn't do group projects."

"Sure, she does."

"No, she doesn't." Juliette straightened a bit, her smile dropping. "She literally talks her way out of having to do any work with other people. She brags about it all the time!"

"I do *not.*" Val smacked her forehead when she realized what she'd said. "I mean, *she* doesn't. I've never heard her say anything like that. She was perfectly happy to work with me."

The sly smile returned to Juliette's face as she looked Val up and down. "Of course she was, you're hot!"

Val sighed and put her face in her hand. "Juliette…"

"Oh, you even know my name!"

"I'm too old for you, okay? Stop—" Val looked up when she heard footsteps. There was Sam, looking for all the world like he belonged in her body when he didn't. Glancing back at Juliette, she shooed her away.

Once she was gone, Sam came closer and said, "What's up?"

Val motioned to the front door, and he followed her out to the porch. As soon as the door was closed, Val pulled out the paper. "Here you go. I rewrote my argument in a larger, special dyslexia font."

"What…what kind of font?" he asked as she took the paper.

"You know," she said as he opened it up. "There's a… You've never seen this before? It's Dislexie. It's supposed to help."

"Oh." Sam looked at the paper, his eyebrows drawn in as he read the words. "Wow. Thanks, Val."

Val shook her head. She should have been thanking *him* but what popped out of her mouth was, "How do you function in school without extra support like this?"

Clenching his jaw, Sam folded the paper back up and said, "I do get extra support. And Tony helps a lot. Is there anything else I can do for you tonight?"

Val's heart fell. Why couldn't she ever say the right thing? "I guess not."

"I'll see you tomorrow then." With that, Sam went back into the house, and she had no choice but to go back to his life.

# Chapter Seventeen

Sam sighed into the paper Val had given him. He hadn't even attempted to read it. He knew it would be filled with words and concepts and thoughts that he couldn't comprehend. Val was too smart for him, smart enough to know things about his own learning disability that he didn't even know. Supposedly anyway.

Out of curiosity, he took one little peek. The words didn't quite dance as much as he was used to. His brain hurt a little less and on top of that, all the arguments she gave in favour of having incinerators were the same ones he would use if he were in the debate. Which…he technically now was. He could do this.

He folded up the paper just as Mrs. Davis called him. Or rather, she called Val, but only Sam was available. Dragging his feet towards the sound of her voice, he found her in the front hall, jangling her keys impatiently.

"Come on," she said. "Don't want to be late."

He didn't want to go at all, let alone be on time. But he had no choice, so he followed her sullenly out of the house and into her car. As he buckled in, she turned on the radio with a huff.

"Your dad always turns off my music," she said. "It's not my fault he doesn't have good taste."

Sam laughed as Tina Turner's "Proud Mary" pumped through the speakers. He liked just about any type of music but could see why Mr. Davis might turn this off. Instead, he sang along quietly, which was…surprisingly enjoyable. He never would have been able to sing along so easily with his own voice.

"Is that…*singing* I hear?" Mrs. Davis said suddenly, her voice laced with mirth.

"No," Sam said quickly.

"I haven't heard you sing in forever!"

He pursed his lips. He should have guessed that Val didn't sing, not even along to her mom's favourite music in the car.

"Ah, I ruined it," Mrs. Davis said softly. "I'm sorry. I never should have said anything. I just love your voice, but I know you don't care about that kind of thing."

Sam smiled. Mrs. Davis seemed like such a nice lady. It couldn't hurt to give her a little taste of something sweet. So he opened his mouth and sang louder, boisterously enough for Mrs. Davis to join in. And boy, did she have quite the voice.

The song hadn't finished by the time Mrs. Davis parked, but Sam wasn't in any rush to get out. Not until they finished rolling on the river together. When the song ended, Mrs. Davis laughed and put an arm around Sam's shoulder to squeeze him.

"That was delightful. Thank you, sweetie."

"You're welcome…Mom." It felt weird to say. Sam hadn't even talked to his own mother in a long time, possibly even close to a year now. But Mrs. Davis smiled brightly at him, love shining in her eyes for…Val. Not him.

"Thanks for the ride," he said quickly before practically jumping out of the car.

He was in no position to be thinking about his mom. If he ever saw her again, she wouldn't recognize him like this. She probably wouldn't even recognize him in his own body, so it was a moot point.

Sam went into the nursing home, inappropriately named Sunny Meadows since there was barely any lawn to speak of and the sun was already descending. Shrugging off his discomfort, he squared his shoulders and tried to fake his confidence.

"Valerie, hi!" the nice receptionist at the desk called cheerfully. She had a pair of horn-rimmed glasses on a chain, which she took to perch on her nose. "Elsa has asked for you this evening if you want to go see her. She's in her room."

Sam smiled tightly and said, "Which room is she again?"

The receptionist tittered and took her glasses off. "You're so funny, Val. 237. You know that."

Flicking his wrist, Sam forced an airy laugh. "Of course I did. I was just testing you. Have a nice night."

"You, too, deary."

Sam turned. Now all he had to do was figure out which way was room 237. The elevator dinged and when he heard the doors opening, he rushed to get on it with a woman who had a walker filled with stuffed animals. She was humming a song to herself, and she patted each of their little heads while the elevator went up.

On the second floor, the little lady meandered down the hallway, right in the middle and swaying back and forth so Sam couldn't get past her. He had no choice but to walk slowly behind her while watching the door numbers he passed. 233…235…237… The lady stopped there, opened the door and then shuffled inside.

"Elsa?" Sam said in surprise.

"Come in, dear, I have zose cookies you like." Elsa said in a thick Eastern

European accent as she waved her hand impatiently for Sam to follow her.

Sam closed the door behind him and then looked around at the crocheted wonderland he'd stepped into. There were little crocheted designs *everywhere*. Every surface, including the pedestal with the small mirror right inside the door, had a doily. Off to the left was a kitchenette with two handmade dish towels hanging off the oven door handle. Straight through where Elsa led Sam was a living area, with a couch covered in crocheted and knitted blankets. The coffee table had yet another homemade craft, a delicately embroidered tablecloth upon which sat a tray of chocolate-coated ginger cookies. They were the kind Sam *loved*, but pricey enough that Ty never brought them home unless they were on sale.

"Help yourself," Elsa said as she sat on the couch.

Sam didn't need to be told twice. He took two and then sat on the couch with her, sinking in delightfully. Okay, maybe he could be happy staying in Val's body forever if he got to enjoy *this*.

"Here is ze book."

Elsa plopped a thick hardcover book into Sam's lap and the dream was shattered. There was a bookmark somewhere in the middle—unsurprisingly crocheted—and so he flipped to those pages. There was a new chapter, so, after a large bite of his cookie, he started there.

He tried to take Tony's advice and read slowly and deliberately. He didn't have problems with comprehension. In fact, he loved stories! Tony's was shaping up nicely, but he had to admit he'd never *read* Tony's work. Tony read it to him. But Tony wasn't here, and neither was Val. He *had* to do this himself.

After Sam had tripped over several words and had barely made it through the first page, Elsa put her hand on the book. "Somezing is wrong, Valerie?"

Sam nodded, but since Elsa was likely mostly blind, he cleared his throat and said, "Don't worry about it. Let me try again."

Elsa let out a crusty laugh and took the book from him, carefully replacing the bookmark. "I never vorry, my dear. But let's talk. Vhat is bozering you?"

How was he supposed to explain what was wrong without saying what was wrong? What would Valerie do? "There's this boy." No, she probably wouldn't have phrased it that way but he'd already said it.

"Ah. It is always a boy."

Sam chuckled. "It's not like that. We're just supposed to work together and he's…not easy to work with."

"Have you tried giving him ze ginger cookies?"

Sam almost laughed out loud, but Elsa's question was so genuine he didn't want to offend her. "No, I haven't. You think that would work?"

Elsa shrugged. "Ze vay to a man's heart is always through his stomach."

Sam could agree with that as he polished off the cookies he'd grabbed. That would work on him, but he wasn't so sure about Val. "It's a little more complicated than that, but I guess it's worth a try."

"Aha." Elsa rose while Sam watched in confusion. She ambled over to the kitchen while he waited more or less patiently. When she came back, she had a sealed bag full of the cookies. "Here you go. This vould bend any man's vill."

Sam's eyes lit up. Val was no man, but he would accept the gift anyway. Maybe he would even share it with her. "Thank you, Elsa. That's *so* nice."

"You don't have to stay today," Elsa said kindly. "Go get your man."

Sam smiled as his cheeks heated up. There was no reason he should have that reaction to what Elsa said. He certainly wasn't out to "get" anyone, let alone Val. Plus he'd come for Val's sake.

"Actually, can I read you something else?" He barely waited for Elsa to nod before pulling out the paper Val had given him. He hadn't had a chance to read the whole thing yet and now seemed like the perfect time. "This is for a debate I'm doing on Saturday. I have to argue in favour of incinerators."

"*Ugh.*" Elsa's whole face puckered up in disgust. "Ve vill burn ze whole vorld down."

"Yeah, I know," he said reluctantly. "But I didn't get to choose which side I'm on, so I'll see if I can make this convincing."

He stood up and began pacing as he read from the paper. "Incinerators. Man-made machines to dispose easily of the world's trash. Imagine if we didn't have piles of refuse littering the ground, filling ditches, polluting the oceans. Wow." Val was right. This font made the words feel far less scrambled up than normal. How had she known?

It was still slow going, but he played it off like he was really trying to drive home the point. Elsa nodded along as he read and when he was finished she applauded for him. Laughing, he bowed for her.

"I still do not like it, but your speech is…very nice." Elsa nodded again. "Put some life into it, and you vill be fine."

"Thanks, Elsa, that helps a lot."

"Ze ginger cookies vill help even more." Elsa winked at him. He could only wish cookies could solve this problem.

Sam left shortly after, thanking Elsa once again for the cookies, the advice, and the visit. But he wasn't ready to go back to Val's home. And he missed his best friend. He texted Tony only to find out that Tony was still at the baseball field, by himself, trying so hard to be something he wasn't.

His heart hurting for his friend, Sam rushed straight over. There was Tony whipping a ball haphazardly at the gate. He didn't look like he was practicing though. He looked angry and his aim proved it.

"Tony!" Sam called out.

Tony whirled around and Sam could immediately see the red in his eyes and the tear stains that had dried on his cheeks. Sam rushed to him and looked him over head to toe to make sure he wasn't hurt.

"Stop that," Tony said weakly, pushing Sam away. "I'm *fine.*"

"Then why were you crying?" Sam asked gently.

That just prompted more tears from Tony, which inexplicably made Sam's eyes water, too. "Because I'm a *terrible* athlete."

Sam's eyebrows drew in, and he blinked his tears away. "Well, yeah, but we already knew that."

"But *she's* not!" Tony threw his hands up and slumped to the ground.

As he drew his knees up to his chest, Sam sat next to him and patted his back. "I know, buddy. It's okay."

Tony sniffled and wiped his cheeks with the back of his hand. "It's fine. How's your thing going?"

Sam shrugged. "Well, I'm still not smart and still can't read. But Val gave me her debate argument in this special font. Did you know there's special fonts for dyslexia?"

Tony's shoulders dropped and he rolled his eyes. "Yeah, dude. I've told you that, like, five times. But you always brush me off because you're happy letting people believe you're dumb but pretty when the opposite is quite true."

"*Please.*"

"Well…" Tony smirked. "Maybe not in that body."

"Yeah, you try telling Val that." Sam scoffed and rose again. "Come on, go get your ball and I'll catch. You can make her look like a bad batter but *not* a bad pitcher. Got it?"

"Yes, ma'am," Tony said miserably. But he retrieved his ball anyway and went to the pitcher's mound.

Sam picked up the glove and went behind first base. Shaking his head, he crouched down, ignoring the cracking his knees made when he spread them far apart. "Alright, give me your best shot."

Tony threw the ball, nice and fast. But it went far over Sam's head. Frowning, Sam went to get it and said, "I said give me your *best* shot. Don't just guess. Throw it where you want it to go."

"Easy for you to say." Tony caught the ball Sam tossed to him. "Mr. I-grew-up-with-a-football-star."

"So, pretend you grew up with a football star," Sam said casually. "You're already pretending to be a girl."

Tony huffed and then got into position again. This time, he took his time and aimed better. The ball was a couple of inches off and Sam only had to reach out to catch it.

Grinning, Sam said, "That was way better! See, you can do this."

Tony shook his head and waited for Sam to throw the ball back. "I don't want to do this forever."

"I know. But we'll have to figure that out later."

# Chapter Eighteen

Thursday morning, the four of them each awoke hoping that they'd somehow made it back into their own bodies. But alas, they were still all mixed up, bound together in a twist of fate that had sent their lives into a spiral.

Ana's mother had yet to show her face and Tony was left to make breakfast for himself and Abuela. Val woke to an empty apartment, having no clue where Ty was—not that he ever really felt present for her anyway. Sam woke up to Harrison loudly gargling water right outside his door and Juliette laughing at him. Sam couldn't help it—he laughed, too, because they were being so silly. Val never would have put up with it.

When Ana got up, Maddy met her in the kitchen with a knowing smile. Maddy was kind enough to ask what Ana would like for breakfast and Ana was a bit taken aback. Normally she cooked at home, not the other way around. And she had yet to make a single meal for herself in Tony's body. Clearly, the youngest Cleaver was the golden child.

After breakfast, Ana met the other three at school, and they loosely greeted each other in a weary way before going to their separate classes. How long would this last? Would they have to finish the school year for each other, take each other's exams, and then choose their senior classes for each other? What then—college? Careers? Families? That sounded like to torture to each one of them.

They rejoined at lunchtime but with so many other students around, it was hard to speak honestly about their situation together. Sam asked Val if he could come over after school to practice his debate speech and she enthusiastically agreed.

But Ana didn't need an invitation to her own home, and she firmly told Tony she was coming over to see how…well, *everything* was going. He would have rather not showed her how terrible he was at being her, but he couldn't very well turn her down.

So at the end of the school day, the two pairs said a hasty goodbye and split up. Ana led the way to her own house while Tony sort of dragged his feet behind her. She did tell him to pick up the pace a few times, citing needing to be fast if he wanted to be a good baseball player. He didn't know how to tell her he had no desire to play baseball, well or otherwise.

"I'm telling you, Ana, I practiced with Sam yesterday and it was…" Tony sighed. "Sam won't say it because he's too nice to me, but I'm terrible. Okay? Isn't there any way I can get out of this?"

Ana tried not to let his request fill her with rage. Hadn't they been working on this all week? The game was two days away. All he had to do was not look stupid. "No."

"Please?"

She stopped in the middle of the sidewalk. They were still in the nice part of town near the high school, and she knew it would look odd if anyone stopped to hear their conversation. But she had to make this very clear to him. "Do you want me to stay home on Saturday instead of going to your writing group?"

He shrugged. "Kind of."

"*What?*" Scoffing, she tossed her hands up. "Why would you say that?"

"I kind of was only going because Sam pushed me into it. *He's* the one who wanted me to do it. He was going to come and listen and then he'd still have time to make it to his photoshoot."

"Tony." She gaped at him, trying to deduce if he were really serious. "What is going on? I thought the whole point was you go and share your book with other writers and... I don't know, they all praise you for being smart or something?"

Half his mouth tilted up at her *interesting* assumption. "They *critique* you, yes. That's the point."

"Okay, great! I'll do that."

"Yeah, I don't want that. I was going to beg off. I'm sure Sam knew it."

When he began walking again, something unidentifiable rose up inside of Ana. Not only did she think he was ridiculous for not wanting her to go to this thing, but if he let her off the hook, then she wouldn't have any leverage to get him to go to her game.

"Hey, wait!" She rushed to catch up to him and took his hand. He stopped abruptly and looked down at their joined hands briefly before giving her a startled look.

"Listen," she said tightening her grasp. "I *really* need you to go to my game, okay? I can't... It's the only... I have nothing else going for me. You understand that, right? You've seen the way I live, you've met my family. If I don't have baseball—" She stopped and swallowed hard. She loved her mom, but this had to be said. "I'm going to end up working with my mom. I love her and I respect her, but I don't want to clean houses for the rest of my life. Do you understand?"

He nodded seriously. "Yeah, I get that. But how is baseball going to help you?"

She sighed and put her face in her other hand. Resisting the temptation to crush Tony's hand, she said, "It really doesn't matter. It could be anything. Anything that shows I'm worth more than just…minimum wage will give me more opportunities. I just happen to be good at baseball. If I lose that, I'll be stuck with a job I hate forever. Or worse—*you* will be."

Tony swallowed hard, once again glancing at their joined hands. He didn't want that life, either. He didn't want to live *Ana's* life, but if he had to then he admitted that she was right and he had to take every opportunity handed to him. "Okay."

"Okay, you'll play?" she pressed.

"Yeah, I'll play your game." He let out a long breath. "I can't guarantee I'll be terrific, but I'll try my best, okay? For you."

She smiled really big, which inexplicably caused butterflies to flutter in his stomach. "Thank you, T. Thank you."

"It's fine."

"You know…" She smiled gently at him. "You could probably do anything you want with your life. But if you really want to be an author, you have to learn to take *some* criticism, right?"

He dropped his gaze. "I know. Sam tells me all the time."

"Right. But…this time, *I* can do it for you. I'm really good at taking criticism."

"Are you really?"

"Sort of."

"So no."

She laughed. "Well, it'll be easier if it's not even my writing."

He couldn't help smiling. "That's a fair point. Alright, yeah, the deal is still on. I'll find the least embarrassing part of my story for you to read. *If* the book isn't totally destroyed."

Guilt gnawed at Ana. No, she hadn't destroyed it. But she'd nearly finished reading everything in it, which Maddy had warned her Tony wouldn't be happy about. She couldn't admit that just yet. "Your book is fine," she said in a tight voice, which probably gave everything away. "I dried it out real good."

"If you say so." He looked down at their hands, still joined together for no discernible reason.

She squeezed his hand and said, "Thank you. You're the best person ever."

"I'm really not," he said weakly.

"You are." She lifted his hand, kissed the back of it, and then dropped it quickly.

His eyebrows drawing in and cheeks reddening, he said, "What…was that?"

"Nothing." She turned away. "Let's go and work on your game."

"Oh…okay."

Ana marched forward, mentally berating herself for her actions. She'd *just* gotten Tony to agree to play her game and then nearly ruined the whole thing by kissing him. What was she thinking? Granted, it was *her* hand she kissed—which just made the whole thing weirder—but his reaction said everything. He would never accept her like this. Why would he? She was *in* his body.

But Tony wasn't thinking that at all. He was still stuck on how Ana had given him the pep talk of a lifetime and how he could suddenly not think of any way to say no to her. Despite not having a single thing in common, not understanding her way of life, and not even really liking the sport, he would do it all for Ana. And for one little kiss. On the back of his hand. A hand that wasn't even his.

"Ana."

"Yup," she said brusquely, not even bothering to look at him.

"You know, if we're stuck like this, you could probably just join a boys' league."

Now she glanced at him and back to the sidewalk that she was trudging down with purpose. "I thought about it. Your body wasn't exactly built to run, but I could probably work with it."

Tony laughed out loud. "If anyone can get my body to do something, it'd be you."

"*What?*"

"That sounded different in my head."

"Okay," she said with laughter in her voice. They turned a corner onto her street and her breath caught in her throat. "*Mami.*"

Tony followed her line of vision as her footsteps quickened. There was an extra car in the driveway of Ana's house. He had no idea where her mother had gone to but evidently she was back. And he had no idea how to act around her.

Ana stopped just short of going up the old porch stairs and motioned for Tony to precede her. Of course, it would look weird it anyone saw Ana going into the house first. Tony went ahead and let them in and was immediately greeted by an older, but still lovely, version of Ana. Ana's mom had thick, curly hair and was a bit shorter than Ana. But her eyes, nose, and lips were almost exactly the same. The resemblance was unmistakeable.

Her mom threw her arms around Tony and hugged him so tightly he could barely breathe while she said some soft Spanish words into his hair.

"Missed you, too," he said when he got the chance.

Señora Dellagusta let go and finally gave Ana a cursory glance. Looking back at Tony, she said, "*¿Quién es?*"

"Oh, I'm just a friend," Ana said, extending her hand. "Tony."

"Oh." Her mom's eyebrows rose as she shook Ana's hand. "You speak Spanish?"

"He really doesn't," Tony said quickly, wishing Ana would stop making him look like he could. This situation was bad enough.

"That's right," Ana said in a heavily disappointed tone, her gaze never leaving her mom. "That's why I'm here. So, uh, Ana can help me learn."

Her mom grunted in an unimpressed way and they both shifted on their feet, wondering if she'd see right through that lie. "Well…okay. Davide said you weren't feeling well, Ana. Are you still going to play your game?"

"I'm fine," Tony said, trying to give her a smile. "I wouldn't miss it for anything."

"Good, good." Señora Dellagusta shook a finger in Ana's face. "Don't you dare distract her. She has important things to do."

"Got it," Ana said. Inside, she was both laughing at her mom's admonition and cringing that Tony had to see that.

"Okay, I have to go, *mija*. Abuela has an appointment." Her eyes narrowed briefly at Ana. "Be good."

"We will," Tony said in a voice that hinted at attitude.

Señora Dellagusta's eyes became tiny slits, but she had no time to answer him as Abuela ambled into the hallway. They kissed Tony goodbye on both cheeks while ignoring Ana. Once they had stepped through the door, Tony wiped his cheeks with the heels of his hands.

"Ugh, *why* is there so much kissing in your family?"

Ana shrugged. "Mom's been gone for almost two weeks. She misses me. I missed her, too. Can't you try to act like you love my family?"

He put his hand on his hip. "I love my family, too, but we're not that affectionate."

"What, you don't like a little kissing, T?" she asked in a teasing voice.

"Not like *that*."

They glanced at each other and then quickly away again. Spying a much-needed aid, Ana picked up the bat, ball, and glove Tony had left by the shoe mat last night.

"Let's just do this," she said, banishing all thoughts of kissing from her mind. She wouldn't be doing that with anyone in *this* body, and helping each other was their best chance of getting back to normal.

# Chapter Nineteen

While Val wouldn't normally have tolerated that much affection from her own family, she would have given anything to have them crush her with their love. But they never would with her looking like this. So instead she found herself trailing behind Sam as they headed to his apartment.

Sam led them a way she wasn't used to, one she would honestly never use if she were in her own body. They didn't exactly live in the rough part of town but it was close enough. In fact, Val cringed when her feet crunched over freshly broken bottle glass. She looked down, only to discover it was *two* bottles, surrounded by five or six cigarettes and even a broken lighter. She shuddered to think what could have happened to create such a mess.

Sam, for his part, seemed completely nonplussed. He even expertly rounded the rusty corner of a blue garbage bin that was overflowing with bulky black garbage bags without even looking at it. Val pinched her nose as they went past and that brought them into the alley next to Sam's building. She would *not* be taking this route again.

As they stepped through the front door—which remained unlocked and sometimes was even left propped open by a cinder block—Val sighed in relief. She felt moderately safer inside knowing she would soon be in a somewhat familiar home, even if it did belong to the Dekker boys. She would take it over that creepy alley.

Val, who had taken possession of Sam's keys along with his body, opened the door of the apartment for them. It was dark inside with all the lights off and the curtains closed. As she flicked the lights on, her gaze darted towards Ty's bedroom door.

"Don't worry, he's not home," Sam said when he noticed Val looking around. "This is his busy day, so we're good."

After making a beeline for his bedroom, he stopped abruptly at the doorway. "What...happened?"

"Oh." Heat rose in Val's cheeks. She'd almost forgotten about rearranging his room in a frenzy. "It felt better this way."

"But you've thrown off the feng shui."

"The feng... Are you kidding me? Do you really believe in that stuff?"

Sam sat on the edge of his bed, frowned at the open window, and bounced up and down a couple of times. "Yes?"

"Sam." Val huffed and stood in front of him with her arms crossed over her chest. "Can we please focus? You have to be at my debate tourney in two days."

"Hmm..." Sam looked her up and down, his frown turning thoughtful. "Oh, that's a good pose. Yeah, I totally see it. Can you push my sleeves up?"

She looked at his arms and said, "What?"

"My... The sleeves *you're* wearing." He flicked his hand in the general direction of her forearms. "Do that thing girls like and just push up 'em all the way up to the elbow."

"Okay..." she said slowly before complying.

"That's good! Now cross your arms again. And now turn your right leg out and—oh!" Sam hastily grabbed Val's phone, since he'd been borrowing it all week long and held it up. "Okay, that's great. Perfect, actually. I'm gonna take your picture so you can remember this pose on Saturday."

"With *my* phone?" she said. "Why?"

He shrugged. "It's in my hand already. Oh, man, keep that look on your face. That's totally my aesthetic."

"Even though everyone calls you Sunny D?" she asked, half appalled, half interested.

"I can't help what people call me." He crouched down and took one last picture before sitting on the bed again. "I mean, they've been calling me Val all week, so…"

She chuckled and finally dropped her pose, pushing her sleeves back down if only so she didn't have to unnecessarily see his forearms. "Sam, can you please read the debate speech for me?"

Reluctantly, Sam nodded and pulled out the paper. He'd read it quite a few times after his visit with Elsa and every time, he let the points sink deeper in. He hadn't memorized it—yet—but he was still confident he could. He'd at least read it enough times that he only tripped over a couple of words, which he admitted to her he didn't even know how to pronounce out loud.

"Demagogue," she said for him after he'd tried a couple of times.

"What does it mean?" he asked, feeling terribly uncomfortable.

"It's like…a leader who follows fads and popular opinions to win votes," she explained.

"As opposed to…"

She dropped her gaze, wondering why he'd ask *that*. "As opposed to one who takes a clear and consistent stance, unwavering in their political and moral standards."

"Unwavering." He smiled suddenly, shaking his head a bit. "I don't think any of them are, but if you ever ran for something, I'd totally vote for you."

"Really?" She lifted an eyebrow. "Because I ran for student council last year against Andi Rowen and lost spectacularly because her campaign involved giving out cupcakes from her mom's bakery."

"Oh, yeah, those were good cupcakes!" Sam's smile grew and then he subsequently lost it when he saw the look on Val's face. "But she's a total demagogue. Got it."

"I wanted more comfortable, ergonomic chairs in the computer lab," she said, her eyes welling up with the pain of that loss. "And access to online resources for every kid in the school so no one fell behind. Why did nobody like that?"

He shrugged. "It sounds more boring than cupcakes."

"*Sam.*"

"I'm sorry, but it does." He gave her a tiny smile. "For what it's worth, *I* voted for you."

Her frown lightened. "You did?"

"Yeah. I really wanted those chairs, too."

"Oh." She shifted, leaning back on her elbows. "So, what do you actually think of my speech?"

Sam bit his lip and looked away which wasn't a good sign to her. "I'll be honest," he said as he stared out the open window. "I haven't even gotten around to understanding it."

"What do you mean? I thought you said you read it a few times."

"Well, yeah." Shrugging, he looked back at her. "So I could make sure all the words were there in my head, so I could say them all properly. I got the gist—garbage shouldn't be filling up landfills and stuff."

"So, you did understand it."

"Sort of? It's just got so many words. Ones you probably don't need." He licked his lips again when she let out a disappointed sigh. "Val, wouldn't your argument be stronger if you just put it in plain language that everyone can understand?"

She clenched her jaw. "It's *strongest* when it uses the best words to match the meaning and tone."

"Maybe tone it down then."

"*Ugh.*" She tossed her hands in the air. "This must be how Matthew Bellamy felt when he wrote 'Uprising.' Like none of his friends could understand him simply because he wanted to state things a certain way."

Sam sat up straighter. Ignoring the fact that she'd compared her speech to a brilliant piece of lyrical writing and that she'd loosely referred to her and Sam as friends, he latched onto the one thing he did love about what she said. "Are you seriously a Muse fan?"

Hesitating, she said, "Isn't everyone?"

"*No.*" He quickly pulled out her phone. "And I don't believe you."

"I...am a Muse fan," she quietly admitted. "A *big* one."

"Prove it."

Before she could ask what he meant, music sprang from her phone. He turned it to max volume while she shook her head. "No."

"*Yes,*" he said with laughter in her voice.

"I...can't." It was such a long intro, they hadn't even gotten to the lyrics yet. "I can't actually sing in his key."

Sam snorted. "*I* can."

She only had a few of measures to decide, but she couldn't *not* sing along to one of her favourite songs. And it turned out Sam was right—his voice was much better suited to the opening lines, which in her natural voice she would typically sing up an octave. But the longer she sang, the more his smile widened. She'd impressed him simply by knowing the lyrics.

And when he sang along with her to the chorus, she knew then and there that someday she might get Sam out of her body but she would never get him out of her head.

The thought was scary and her singing faltered. She almost asked him to stop the song, but then he started playing air guitar during the second verse and really got into it, and she didn't have the heart to stop him. Plus, she didn't know anyone who knew this song like she did. She couldn't stop now.

Sam played some more air guitar during the interlude and Val couldn't help playing air drums along with him. When the last chorus came along, he grasped her forearms and they sang right into each other's faces, which wasn't as unpleasant as it might have been had it been anyone else. Val even sang the lower harmonies to his melody.

They ended the song in laughter, their hands still wrapped tightly around each other's elbows. Val let go first but only because she realized how hard she'd been holding onto him. Sam didn't seem to mind as he sat next to her on the bed.

"Wow," he said as he gazed into his own smouldering eyes. "I had no idea you were so cool under all that...hmm...*rhetoric*."

"Oo, good word." She chuckled. "But I'm really not. And don't you dare tell my mom you caught me singing." When his only response was to bite his lip and look away, she nudged his shoulder with hers. "Hey, what's up? That was a joke."

Nodding, he turned back to her. "Yeah, I kind of have a confession to make. I sang Tina Turner in the car with your mom."

Val let out a short bark of laughter. "Seriously? She must have loved that."

"She did." Quietly, he added, "I did, too. She's a cool mom. Your whole family is...nice." It was a lame finish and not what he meant, but he didn't want to open up too much.

She could hear the longing in his voice, no matter how much he tried to hide it. "You don't...sing with your mom ever?"

He shook his head, his lips pursed tightly. "I haven't even seen my mom in over a year," he whispered. Feeling like that was too much of an admission, he cleared his throat. "Anyway, I'm sorry if I wasn't supposed to do that. It just happened. And I like Tina Turner."

"Of course," she said, catching his change of topic. "What's not to like?"

"Right? Your mom's right, though," he said softly. "You do have a nice voice. I can see why she likes hearing it."

She shrugged, her shoulder lightly bumping against his. "I don't really sing."

"You clearly do," he said with laughter in his voice.

She looked into his teasing eyes. "Okay, well, I don't *perform*. Not like you. I don't have your kind of charisma."

"Hey, I don't perform either."

"Modeling...*isn't* a performance?"

"No?"

She got up and took the pose she'd done earlier for him and then stared at him for a few seconds waiting for him to react. He didn't. "Is this not performing?"

He laughed and said, "No. That's just standing."

She dropped her arms and chuckled, too. "Okay, okay. There's nothing special about you or what you do. Is that what you want to hear?"

"Yeah," he said, but he didn't sound like he meant it.

"Oh, come on," she said. "You know that's not true. Everybody likes you. No matter where you go, you'll always find a friend and you'll always be able to get around. You could probably literally travel the world and be totally fine. And I mean, look at me." She gestured to her head. "You have a face for TV, but I'm sure you knew that."

He rolled his eyes even as her compliments warmed him from the inside out. "Yeah, that's nice until I run out of people to help me. I'm not like you. You don't need anyone else. You can do whatever you want whenever you want, and you'll figure it all out on your own. I wish I had even a little bit of that."

Chuckling, she came forward and took his hands, lifting them up in front of his face. "You kind of do."

He looked at their hands and then into her eyes. "Yeah, I guess I do."

Smiling, she dropped his hands. "Can I hear the speech one more time?"

"Sure."

He stood up while she sat down again. She found he couldn't stand still while reading the speech, and instead needed to pace back and forth. It would be a problem if they gave him a mic on a stand, but she could worry about that later. For now, she would just watch Sam.

It was so uncanny, the way his personality propelled him forward, how the inflections in the speech she'd written were all his. She would have read it differently, but she didn't exactly have time to teach him how to speak exactly like her. Instead, she had to do what he said he'd been doing all along and rely on another person. She would just have to trust Sam. She had no other choice.

# Chapter Twenty

Val made Sam read her speech two more times while tweaking his inflections every once in a while. He didn't think having just the right emphasis made all that much difference, but he was too afraid of her to say so. Besides, after that, she let him pose her however he wanted. And some of the poses were downright painful.

"How, exactly, does this make me look sexy?" Holding the lapels of her polo shirt with just the tips of her pointer fingers and thumbs, she'd carefully turned her hands out. Then she perched on the edge of Sam's desk chair and leaned forward at the most awkward angle.

"I never said it had to be sexy." He snapped a pic and then smiled. "Oh, but that does look good. Look!"

She released the awful pose as Sam came closer to show her the picture. She... Well, he... They looked good in that pose. Really good. Val hadn't been lying when she'd told him he was the most handsome boy she'd ever met. His skin was flawless, his eyes smouldered just right, and his hair was perfectly thick and dark. That, mixed with his nicely shaped lips—which look good in both a frown and a smile—made him quite honestly a perfect model.

But considering how he'd reacted when she'd told him that, she chose not to repeat it. He likely knew it anyway considering how he always flaunted his goods to the girls at school. So, why then, when Val had complimented him, had it ruffled so many of his feathers?

She had no time to ask. Realizing how late in the day it had gotten, she suggested he go "home" and have dinner with her family.

"And definitely don't tell them I was here with you," she added.

His eyebrows drew in. "Why not?"

She could see the hurt in his eyes, and she quickly explained, "I just don't want them to think there's more between us than there actually is."

"I get it," he said in a tight voice. "They wouldn't approve."

"It's not like that."

"It's fine, Val." He gave her a smile that didn't reach his eyes and headed for the bedroom door.

She couldn't stop him. It was his apartment, and he had no choice but to take her body with him. When they stepped outside and heard clanging sounds in the kitchen preceded by footsteps towards them, they both stop in their tracks. Ty poked his head out of the kitchen, took one look at Sam, and flashed a charming smile.

"Hey, there," he said. "You staying for dinner?"

"Oh, I—I didn't know you were here," Sam stammered. "I thought you'd be out till later."

Ty lifted an eyebrow. "Don't know why you'd think that since we don't even know each other. Unless Sam was *hoping* I'd still be out."

"*No*," Val said urgently. "Really, no. She's just…being weird. And she's going home now. Her family needs her. Bye."

She put her hand on Sam's back and gave him a light push. But he didn't take kindly to it, and he scowled at her as he whispered, "You don't have to push me."

"I didn't," she hissed under her breath. "But I will if you don't leave."

"Alright, alright." Sam took one last longing glance at Ty—which was sure to be misinterpreted later—and finally saw himself out.

As soon as the front door clicked shut, Ty turned to Val with a grin. "Wow, she's cute!"

"Uh huh," she said, in no mood to be complimented by him.

"Seriously. And I haven't heard you sing in forever." Ty bobbed his eyebrows.

Val groaned. "You were here for that?"

"Yup." He chuckled. "Maybe one day you'll actually go on the stage like Maddy thinks you should."

"What do you care?" she asked.

His smile dropped. "What do you mean?"

"I mean…you don't care about your brother," she blurted out. "You're the only person he's got left if this world and you just…treat him like he's *there*. But not like you care."

His eyes narrowed. "*Excuse me?* What makes you think I don't care about you?"

She shook her head, pursing her lips. "You don't care what he does or where he goes and whether he does well in school. You don't care about his relationships or whether he's heading in the right direction. He doesn't even know there are more resources for his dyslexia! So, why should you care if he goes on stage or not?"

"Sam…" His eyebrows drew in tightly. "Why are you saying all this?"

She shook her head. What would it matter if she told him the truth? It's not like he'd believe her. "I'm not Sam. And I said it because it's true. Isn't it?"

"*No*, it's not." Leaning against the doorframe, he slung his dishtowel over his shoulder and crossed his arms. "Who are you and who do you think you are to say that kind of stuff?"

"My name is Valerie," she said quietly.

"That pretty girl who just left?" He jutted his thumb towards the door. When she simply nodded, he frowned at her. "Okay, well, I've never met you before and I'm guessing you don't know Sam very well. So I really don't owe you an explanation. But since you seem to be stuck in his body, you should know that the *real* truth is that our mom ditched us years ago and our dad is an angry alcoholic. That's why he has no one but me.

"When I moved out, I had two options—live on my own by my own rules or take Sam with me so he could have just *one* person in his corner. I didn't have to work two jobs and go to school on a scholarship so I could afford an apartment for *both* of us. But I did. And I never asked him to get a job so he can focus on school and do what *he* wants."

She swallowed hard, wondering if she should backtrack now, but Ty apparently wasn't finished.

"Unlike our parents," he continued, "*I* want him to be able to live his dream, whatever that is. But I'm not his dad, so no, I don't set rules for him. I love him and I want him to be happy and you have no right to judge me for whatever you think is going on here. Also, I saw you ruined the feng shui in his room, but I didn't say anything about that because I figured *Sam* did that. Anything else you want to say to me?"

She shook her head. Maybe she *had* been too quick to judge. After all, Sam had already told her about his mom, and it was a safe assumption that his dad didn't want to look after him either. Still, it was concerning that Ty hadn't even really addressed the fact that Val had told him she wasn't his brother.

"Are you sure?"

She lifted her gaze to look right into his angry eyes. "Do you really believe we switched bodies?"

He forced a shrug. "Sam would never say that stuff to me, so yeah."

Tears inexplicably filled her eyes. Maybe it was from relief of having told someone else, or maybe it was just that she was so done with this week. Either way, one tear had already slipped down her face, and she brushed it quickly away. "I don't want to do this. I don't want to live Sam's life. He's a nice boy, and I'm sure he'll be great wherever he goes, but this isn't what I wanted for me, and I just—"

"Oh, um—" Ty dropped his arms and his frown softened. "No, don't cry. It's fine. Everything will be fine."

"You don't know that!"

"Yes, I do." He came closer and held an arm out. "Do you…want a hug?"

She nodded and came closer to him. It was awkward for both of them, but Val still appreciated the gesture. At home, she hardly ever let anyone hug her anymore, but maybe that would change…if she ever got her body back.

As he let go of her, he said, "Is he supposed to be doing something important for you sometime soon? He has a terrible memory so he might need a lot of help with that."

"*What?*" she squeaked. "He promised he'd memorize my debate speech for me because he didn't want to have to read it on the spot. Now you're telling me he *can't* do that?"

"Oh, I mean…" Ty cringed. "I'm sure he'll do his best. Are you going to his photoshoot?"

"Yes," she said begrudgingly.

"Don't mess it up." He didn't sound unsympathetic, but he clearly wasn't the type to hold anything back. "This is a big break for Sam and if it leads to more jobs, he might actually give me something that resembles rent."

Reckless rebellion rose up in her and she said, "He could be doing a lot more with his life than just modeling. I know you think I don't know him, but I do. Well enough to know there's a bigger life out there for Sam."

"That might be true—" he paused to give her a tight smile "—but it's what Sam likes. And he feels like he's good at it. So."

She nodded. She'd heard him loud and clear. Do Sam's thing, and don't interfere. Easier said than done. "You could at least have looked a little harder for resources for him…"

Ty sighed and stepped away from her. "I didn't sign up to be a dad, okay? I didn't even know he had trouble reading until Maddy pointed it out and then Tony took over for me. And by the way, I know about the resources and so does Sam. But like I said, he's got a terrible memory. So good luck with that, Valerie."

She let out a long breath. Luck was seemingly the only thing she could bank on at this point.

*   *   *

Ana and Tony practiced pitching until Tony's shoulder was sore and Ana's voice was hoarse from yelling instructions at him. He was the one who stopped her—not because he was in pain, but because he didn't want her to lose her voice. After all, if she was going to read for him in two days, it would be no good to have no voice.

Putting her hand on his right shoulder, she massaged it gently. "Put some ice on this when you get home, okay? You worked a little too hard."

"Too hard," he muttered, shaking her hand off. "You're welcome. Go and have some lemon tea with honey."

"Alright, Grandma," she sassed.

She watched him walk away, rubbing his shoulder as he went. Why couldn't he have just let her do that for him? She knew where the tense spots were, plus then he wouldn't have to twist awkwardly just to get a massage.

She shook her head. No matter. She would go and have his tea and finish transcribing his book. She only had a few pages left. Then she could show it to him, and he would be grateful, and they could pick out the best part for her to read. A perfect plan.

It didn't take her long to finish, after which she had dinner with Tony's family, including his two sisters. Stella went on and on about some company that wanted to endorse her—though it sounded like an MLM to Ana—while she ate quietly, wondering how Tony was. Maddy helpfully redirected the conversation whenever anyone tried to engage Ana in a topic she knew nothing about.

It was nice, though, how Stella kept asking Tony's opinions on things. Ana didn't know Stella well enough to have advice for her, and she didn't know what Tony's relationship with his oldest sister was like. But Stella genuinely seemed to care what he thought. Ana did her best to answer.

"Oh! Are you going to Sam's photoshoot?" Stella asked. "I'm sure they'll let you in to watch if you don't get in the way. You can call yourself his entourage or something."

"And it's before the reading anyway," Maddy said helpfully. "So it's not like you won't be able to."

Ana smiled gratefully at that and wondered if Val would even want her there. "I wouldn't miss Sam's photoshoot for the world," she said.

It was unfortunate that Tony *would* miss it. He and Sam had been looking forward to this day. Tony was happy for Sam's "big break" and Sam was just happy that he had convinced Tony to come out of his shell and show off his talent. Now the day belonged to someone else, and it wasn't at all comforting knowing the girls were also missing something huge. What a mess.

# Chapter Twenty-One

Tony was still sore when he got up. He knew he'd overdone it with Ana yesterday, but he had no choice. He either had to get good at playing baseball or drop out. And he wasn't prepared to drop out of her game. Did he want to play for her forever? No. But he could power through this weekend for her sake.

And he could get through meals with her family for her. Despite having taken Spanish the last two years, he couldn't keep up with her family. Her dad spoke a little slower, but when Mami and Abuela got going, they were way too fast. Tony caught snippets here and there, but Abuela was also very confused about things, which made Tony extra confused.

Davide was the only person who consistently spoke English to him, but every time they did, Señor Dellagusta frowned in disapproval. But if Tony were really stuck in this body forever, Ana's family would have to be real cool about his terrible Spanish.

"Ana." Abuela's voice was gravelly and yet somehow warm as she pushed a bowl of cubed watermelon towards Tony.

He pulled the bowl closer towards himself. "Gracias." That much, at least, he could handle.

And Ana could certainly handle Tony's two fast-talking sisters. She was no stranger to these types of conversations. They ran rampant through her baseball team, in the locker rooms at school, in her classes even. They talked about boys, hair, nail polish, celebrity couples. Sometimes they talked about their goals and aspirations, but never like Ana would have chosen.

Ana wanted to go pro. Maybe become a World Series champion or play across the globe. Even the others on her team didn't share this dream, which she understood. Becoming a pro athlete was hard. Harder still when you had no control over your own body.

And so, the conversations that whirled around her had always been adjacent, never directed at her. And Ana was fine with that. She didn't need close friends to get to where she wanted to go. She only needed herself.

And, well…Tony.

Not that she *needed* Tony, but she…needed him. Oh. He would never go for her like this. And if they ever switched back, he would probably never want to look at her again. Not that he was even looking in the first place. This train of thought was a fruitless endeavour.

"Tony, what's wrong?" Stella asked, her lips turned down in a sweet little frown. "I thought you loved my smiley face pancakes."

Maddy nodded encouragingly, and Ana smiled at both of them. "They're delicious. I just have…a lot on my mind."

"You mean you're nervous about your reading?" Stella, sounding both patronizing and comforting, bobbed her eyebrows at him. "I told you it'll be fine! You're a great writer. And we'll all be there rooting for you."

Ana swallowed hard and shot a panicked look at Maddy. "You…you will?"

"Mmhmm," Maddy murmured, her eyes wide. "Remember? We all said we'd go, and Sam will be there, too?"

*Sam?* Sam was in Val's body. But Maddy didn't know that. And it didn't matter anyway. Val hardly had any knowledge of Tony's books. "You're right," Ana said with a faked confidence. "It's gonna be great!"

"That's the spirit!" Stella said with a big smile.

Despite not being related to these ladies at all, Ana still appreciated their enthusiasm and support. It was nice for Tony, actually. Maybe they were a bit overbearing at times, but they clearly loved their baby brother and thought the world of him. Of course, Maddy knew her brother wasn't here right now. But she'd done a lot with Ana for Tony's sake and that said even more about her love for him.

It made her miss Davide. He wasn't the most affectionate brother, but Ana preferred him that way. Plus he was the one who had taught her all about baseball. When they were younger, he taught her to hit the ball. But eventually, she wanted to try throwing and when he realized how good she was at that, they'd focused so much on it that Ana was now her team's ace. And she never wanted to look back.

Emotion suddenly clogged the back of her throat and she could barely swallow her next bite of pancake. She pushed her plate away and excused herself and rushed off to Tony's room. Only when the door was firmly shut did she let herself cry. She'd been keeping it together so well, but she couldn't any longer.

What if she was stuck like this forever? Would she ever see her mother and father, Davide, or Abuela again? Tony's sisters were nice enough but Ana wanted her own family, her own life back. Baseball! She missed the rough feel of the ball as she found the perfect grip for it, and the smoothness of her bat as she waited for a pitch. Would she ever play again?

There was a knock on the door and as Ana quickly brushed away the tears on her cheeks, she called out, "Yeah?" in a thick voice.

"It's Maddy."

Ana opened the door and Maddy immediately frowned sympathetically at her. "Oh, I'm so sorry." Maddy put her arms around Ana, and Ana couldn't have stopped her even if she wanted to. "Everything's gonna be okay."

"If you say so."

"I do." Maddy pulled back and smiled at her. "Just do your best and things will turn out. I promise."

Ana shook her head, but she didn't have time to argue. Not if she wanted to get to school on time. So Tony's academic rep didn't get marred. What was even the point of all this?

At school, Ana sought out Val, as it seemed natural to do since Tony and Sam were always seen together anyway. Val smiled at her, a rare sight even though Sam was generally a smiley person.

"Did you know you have to go to my book reading?" Ana said by way of greeting.

Val's smile fell a bit. "No. Sam didn't mention it."

"Of course he didn't," Ana said. "He has a terrible memory." When Val cringed, she asked, "What's wrong?"

"He said he'd memorize my debate speech, but everyone keeps mentioning how awful his memory is."

"I'm sure it'll be fine," Ana said quickly. "He knows how important this is. Anyway, you don't have to come see me…read a book. It's not a big deal."

Val shrugged. "I'll come. I'm interested now to know more about Valentino."

Ana smiled. Now that she'd gotten through Tony's handwritten book, she knew she had to read the ending…whenever he got around to writing it. "Then I'll come to your photoshoot."

Val frowned uncertainly but Ana just laughed.

Ana was anxious to get through her day. She wanted so badly to watch Tony pitch again—as bad as it was—but she still had to show him his own writing. At least he seemed relieved at the end of the day when she told them they were going to his house.

"Come on, T, we have to pick what I'm going to read for you." She practically had to drag him into his own room. "And I just found out your whole family's gonna be there. You could have told me!"

He shrugged. "I told you already my initial plan was to just bail."

She sighed and then couldn't help smiling at him. "We're not doing that. Come on, I have a surprise for you."

"What is it?" he asked in a less than impressed tone as he slumped down on his bed.

"I know you were disappointed about your book getting wet, soo…" She opened his laptop and spun it to face him. "I typed it up!"

"What?" he said, his whole face paling.

"I didn't want you to lose all your work, so I typed it to make sure your story was safe." When he didn't answer and just stared at the words on the screen, she added, "It was a bit hard since your handwriting's messy and it was smudgey, but Maddy helped, too."

"Ana," he breathed. His throat felt like it was constricting, his mouth gone dry. "You...you read my book? And you let all those people read it, too?"

Her eyebrows drew in at his ungrateful response. "I...had to. It was the only way to fix my mistake. You understand that, don't you?"

"I can't believe you read it…"

She rolled her eyes at him. "I even added to it!"

"*What?*" he squeaked. He floundered for words, trying to express how much she shouldn't have even touched his book, let alone added to the story he'd crafted himself.

"Yeah, I just thought… Look, if Valentino is going to kiss Sparkle, she's gonna hit him for it." Ana shrugged like she couldn't think of any other explanation.

His eyes widened. "You made Valentino do *what?*"

Ana's eyebrows drew in, her confusion clearly written on her face. "*I* didn't. You did! Right?"

She picked up his book—while he scoffed at her for touching it once again—and flipped to the page she'd mentioned. "See, here."

As she pointed to a spot on the page, he sucked in a deep breath. "That says he *hissed* in her face. Hissing! Not kissing!"

"*Oh.*"

"*Yeah.*"

"I mean I thought it was weird that he kissed her right in the face, but it's a fantasy story after all, so I figured, like, whatever."

Shaking his head, he took the book out of her hands and slapped it shut. "And what exactly did you write?"

Ana opened his laptop, found that part of the document and sheepishly turned it towards him. He zeroed in on the screen, his eyes narrowing as he read the words that she'd written.

"'He *kissed* her...lips!'"

"Yeah, I changed that because 'kissed her in the face' didn't make any sense. Even for a fantasy story."

"Oh, okay," he said sarcastically. "She slaps him—as she should—and then... *Ana.*"

"What?"

"They kiss *again?*"

She shrugged.

"'He dropped his dagger and put his hands around her neck while his forked tongue—' *Ana.*"

"Well, he has a forked tongue, doesn't he?"

He slammed his laptop shut and shot daggers at her from his eyes. "You're ruining my life. As if *this*—" he gestured back and forth between them "—wasn't bad enough. Now you're turning my book into smut?"

She rolled her eyes. "It's not smut. It's just a very chemically charged kiss between two characters who were definitely asking for it. It's not my fault you don't know your own characters."

"I do know them!" He threw his hands up. "And I know they would *never.*"

"It's *just* a kiss, T. What have you got against them? Why are you so—" She grunted in frustration. "Look, it's not that complicated!"

She grabbed his shoulders and pulled him forward, and before he could even utter a confused protest, she planted her lips straight on his. Or did she plant *his* lips on *her* own? Oh, now that was a little too weird for her liking, and she pulled back as abruptly as she went in.

After a short, awkward silence Tony said in a soft whisper, "That felt pretty complicated."

"Yeah."

"But I didn't hate it."

Her face flushed hot as she realized she didn't hate it either. She dropped her gaze and turned around. "Anyway…let's take the kiss out of the book and pretend I never misread your handwriting."

When she reached for his laptop, he grabbed her hand. She stared at him during the short moment before he leaned in to kiss her gently. He even put his hand up to her face like Valentino might have were he actually in love with Sparkle.

Maybe he *was* in love with her.

"I really don't hate that," Tony whispered against her lips.

"I guess it's not the worst thing," she whispered back. She covered his hand with hers. "Then again, I am just kissing myself."

He chuckled, his breath tickling her cheek. He pulled back to look into her eyes. "You really think Valentino and Sparkle belong together?"

"The tension between them is palpable," she said, instead of telling him she'd had a crush on him for the longest time.

"I guess it can stay." He slid his hand out from under hers and turned to his computer. "I'm sure Sam'll love drawing that. Let's see what other messes you got my characters into."

"Okay," she said quietly.

As he skimmed through the pages, scrolling quickly, Ana chewed her lip. She and Maddy had taken some creative licenses while trying to transcribe the passages they didn't understand or couldn't read. But that wasn't what was on her mind. It was the fact that Tony had kissed her back and was now being quite nonchalant about it.

"Wow," he said when he got to the end of the document. "I can't believe that one scene that you broke and rewrote is the best one in the whole book."

Ana stared at him. "Did you just…read all that? I mean, that quickly?"

"Pretty much."

"You're even more amazing than I originally thought."

He finally turned to her, one eyebrow raised. "I didn't know you thought I was amazing to begin with."

Her gaze fell. "And other times you're just really dumb. Of course I think that!"

Bewildered, he said, "How was I supposed to know? You never talk to me."

"I don't talk to *any* boys!"

"Because we're a little dumb?" he said as a corner of his mouth tipped up.

"Yup."

His smile grew and he reached out to take one of her hands. "What was your favourite part of the book?"

"Hard to say when there's so many gaps for you to fill in." She swallowed hard as she glanced briefly at their hands. "But probably when Valentino finds that special sword."

Tony nodded. "You can read that part, then."

"Are you just going to ignore us kissing?" she burst out.

"For now, yeah." He turned back to the laptop and scrolled casually, looking for the part about the sword.

"Why?"

"Because I'd rather be kissing your actual lips. So maybe if this works and we switch back—" he turned to her and bobbed his eyebrows "—then we can talk about it again."

"That is *such* a Valentino thing to say," she muttered. He merely smirked.

# Chapter Twenty-Two

While Ana couldn't stop thinking about Tony kissing her, Val would never dare think of Sam that way. There was nothing wrong with him. Sam was charming and likeable in his own way. And the fact that he knew what he wanted—even if Val didn't get it—made him all the more desirable. But that was dangerous thinking. All she wanted was to get back into her own life where she knew she wouldn't have to cross paths with him again.

Everyone was convinced that the only way to get her body back was to help Sam with this one thing. And it shouldn't have been that hard. But when Val tried to pose the way she thought Sam should, all of her pictures came out weird. Selfies were bad—she'd never been good at them. Using the camera on a timer was even worse. This seemed impossible.

She would have loved to ask Ana how to go about this, but Ana was probably too busy trying to make Tony resemble a world-class pitcher. Which meant Tony was out, too. And Sam was at her place, having dinner with her aunt and uncle and then hopefully, she *prayed*, memorizing the life out of her speech. That really only left...Ty.

Reluctantly, she left Sam's room and knocked hesitantly on Ty's bedroom door. He answered after a moment, with something between sympathy and irritation in his eyes. "You good?" he asked nonchalantly.

"No, I'm not good!" She threw her hands up. "I've got this gorgeous body and I don't know what to do with it."

Laughter sputtered out of him. "I don't know how to help you with that. I mean, he's my baby brother…"

"I meant—" She sighed as her face flushed hot. "I don't know how to *pose* the body for pictures. I look terrible in every one I've taken."

"Again, I really don't know how to help you with that."

"Please," she whined. "You must have watched him do his thing. I'm sure you know how he poses. I can only do it when he tells me how and right now… He's not available."

Ty groaned, putting a hand up to his head. "I'm trying to write an essay, Valerie."

"Great." She smiled in what she hoped was Sam's charming way. "I'll help you after I'm done this photoshoot."

He stared at her for a moment. "Seriously?"

"Yup. I love writing essays."

Ty put his hand out. "Deal."

Val put her hand in his and he shook it so hard, it flailed all over the place. "First rule," he said, "don't be too rigid and definitely don't be too loose."

"Oh, no…"

"You asked."

"I know."

He let go of her hand. "I think it's really just as easy as following whatever the photographer says. They always know how things will look just right. But Sam's done this before and he's watched a ton of videos, so he's gotten used to how it goes. That's why he poses so naturally. Have you even asked him about it?"

"Not really," she said with a shrug. "He told me the same thing you did, to just do whatever the photographer says. And everyone once in a while, he sees me standing and thinks it's the most amazing thing in the world. Of course, how could you not feel that way when you can see yourself from a distance?"

Ty's eyebrows drew in. "Do you even like Sam?"

"What?" she asked, her face mirroring his.

"You keep talking down about what he likes, what he's good at." He shook his head. "So do you like him? Are you friends?"

"I don't even know him," she said quietly.

"Oh, but you claimed to know him even better than his own brother." A smug smirk replaced his frown. "So which is it?"

"Well, I—" She shifted from foot to foot. "I just— I don't know what I'm supposed to say. It seems like you have your mind made up already."

His smirk softened to a genuine smile as he patted her on the shoulder. "I suggest you go talk to Sam. Like *really* talk to him."

"What good would that do? We still have to prepare for tomorrow and it just feels like nothing will work out."

"I don't know how to tell you this, but… I don't think it matters what happens tomorrow. You're stuck in his body. You might as well find out what he wanted to do with his life and see if that works for you or not."

Val's shoulders drooped. Ty was right, after all. If she was stuck forever, she had to decide for Sam. Not him. She sighed. "Alright, I'll be home later."

"Do what you gotta do."

She nodded. Maybe it was a worthwhile idea. Deciding she didn't want to talk with Sam at either of their houses, she asked if he'd meet her halfway between. The Bridgetown Community Church would do just fine.

Sam agreed to meet her there and she hastily left the apartment. Inwardly, she admitted it was a bit freeing to not have to tell someone where she would be every second of the day. But that just made her feel guilty. If she could tell her parents where she was…they wouldn't believe her anyway. They would probably kick her out of the house and suggest she have her parents take her to the doctor.

Her vision got cloudy, and she wiped at her eyes before the tears could fully form. They could do this. Ty was *so* confident if she just talked to Sam and tried his thing that everything would be okay. But there was no way he could know that for sure.

Val stuck to the main streets instead of Sam's sketchy back alleys to get to the nice little church that was just on the edge of the downtown core. The building, with its tall white steeple, solid oak doors, and sprawling lawn had been plopped down in the middle of nowhere over a century ago. Now it was in the middle of town but had retained its charm and had officially been designated as a heritage building.

She loved the way it looked but couldn't remember ever having set foot in it. And that wouldn't change today. She didn't think the church could help her out of Sam's body.

"Hey."

Now, that wasn't her voice but it was familiar. She whirled to face Ana. "Hey…what are you doing here?"

Ana shrugged. "Tony said Sam said we're meeting here."

Groaning, Val put her face in her hand. "I was supposed to be meeting *Sam* here. Just Sam. So I can figure out *Sam*."

"Ohhhh… You wanted to be alone." Ana bobbed her eyebrows.

"What… No…"

"Hey, I'm here." That was *Ana's* husky voice. "I practised just like you asked me to, Ana."

"Hey, Tony. That's great!" Ana said happily while Val's eyebrows drew in. Tony smiled back at her and Val felt even more confused. Weren't they just as twisted up as she was?

"Any idea where Sam is?" Val asked, irritation seeping into her voice.

Tony just shrugged but his smile never left. "He just said we're all meeting here."

"Val says she wanted to be alone with Sam," Ana said. "I don't know why Sam told us to come."

"Ohhh…" Tony's smile turned sly. "We'll leave then. It's fine."

"No, just—ugh." Val groaned again. "You're making it sound…weird!"

Tony shrugged again and then he looked past her. "Oh, there he is. Hey, Sam!" he shouted as she waved enthusiastically.

"Hey, maybe keep your voice down?" Val anxiously reached out to grabbed Tony's wrist. "People are gonna think it's weird you're calling *me* Sam."

"Oh, right."

Rolling her eyes, she turned around, and then rolled her eyes again even harder. Sam was wearing a grey pencil skirt, a sequined purple shirt, and a red blazer. The blazer wasn't even hers. "Sam…what are you wearing?"

"Oh, this old thing?" he said in a cheeky voice as he joined them. "I tried on a few different outfits for your debate. You have such great clothes. This skirt? And this shirt? Then your mom was *thrilled* when I asked if she had a jacket I could put with it."

Val huffed in indignation while Ana touched the soft velvet of the jacket's sleeves. "Sam. My debate is about how well I can form an argument, not how well I wear a jacket."

He thought about it for a second before saying, "But you *do* wear this jacket well. Your mom thought so, too."

"No, he's right," Ana said. "You look great!"

"Thanks," Sam said cheerfully while Val mumbled it miserably.

"I feel like I'm the only one taking this thing seriously," Val said, staring at each one of them in turn. "I mean, Sam, you *have* been working on the speech, right? You said you'd memorize it!"

"I am working on it," he promised, forcing his face to drop to a more serious, neutral look. "But I can't just do that for hours on end. I took one break to draw, and one break for trying on clothes."

"To draw?"

"Yeah, of course," Sam said. "Once I found out Valentino and Sparkle kiss, I just had to!"

Tony, who had been trying to stay out of the argument, sputtered and elbowed Ana hard. "You told him?"

Ana clutched her side where Tony had stuck his borrowed bony elbow, and said innocently, "You said he'd be excited. I thought we could surprise you with a picture, but Sam can't keep his mouth shut."

"I didn't know it was a surprise," Sam said plainly.

"Wait a minute—" Val held up a hand. "Sparkle, the pink fairy, actually kisses that hulking green guy with—" she pointed to her lips "—huge teeth?"

"Right?" Ana said with laughter in her voice.

Tony stepped closer to Val and glared at her. "How do *you* know about Sparkle and Valentino?"

"Well, after seeing the pictures and then reading the book with Ana, I—"

Tony sucked in a sharp breath. "You read my book, too?"

"You looked at my pictures?" Sam spit out, sounding betrayed.

Both boys, who looked adorable as angry girls, put their hands on their hips and waited for an explanation. Val swallowed hard. She hadn't meant to make either one angry. In fact, she was hoping to make better friends with them, not make enemies of them.

"First of all," she said calmly, holding up a finger, "I was helping Ana make sense of your book. We just wanted to repair the damage she'd done. And second, your art is all over your room, Sam. And…on your desktop." She whispered the last part, knowing that was harder to justify than the pages that had sat right out on his desk.

"You looked at *all* of it?" he asked quietly.

She nodded and he pulled his bottom lip in and turned away. It was clear she'd hurt him, which wasn't her intention. "It's really good, Sam. I couldn't help myself."

"Yeah, like you couldn't help starting an argument with me when I was trying to get my wallet back," he said bitterly.

"Oh, you and your stupid wallet!" She reached into her back pocket and pulled it out. "You want it so badly, take it!" She whipped it at him and he only had a second to try to catch it.

It landed on the ground and he reached down to pick it up while giving her a scowl. "*Hey*! That was a gift from Tony's parents. Be gentle with it."

The wallet. That's what had gotten them into this mess in the first place. That and Ana's bat, which Tony needlessly pointed out. Ana took offense at that, since she still claimed he should have been more careful with his own book.

At that point, the four of them started arguing, talking over each other and nitpicking at the things they hadn't liked the others had done. Even Tony and Sam couldn't keep their judgments to themselves as they felt they each should have done a better job of protecting their best friend's most inner thoughts that had spilled out into their art and words.

None of them were particularly good at presenting their arguments—not even Val, a seasoned debater—and they were suddenly back to where they started in the first place. Uncompromising, unwilling to see the others' sides, and inconsiderate of what they might say.

"Hey!" a voice shouted. But when they ignored it at first, the man shouted again, even louder. "Hey! Stop that!"

All four quieted down and turned to the man in ripped jeans and an old sweater with holes. He didn't look angry, but rather heavily concerned as he met each of their gazes.

"What's going on here?" he asked.

"I'm sorry, who are you?" Val asked, never one to back down from anyone.

"I'm the pastor of this church," he said, jutting his thumb over his shoulder at the quaint white building. "Was working late when I saw you four arguing through my office window. I've taken a lot of courses on body language and I honestly can't tell what's going on here. Are you friends? Enemies? Any of you dating? You're all so confusing."

"We were just...having a discussion, sir," Tony said.

"And we're friends," Sam added. "Friends who just..." He glanced at Val quickly. "Got a little off-track."

"And none of us are dating," Ana said. Then she quietly added, "Though I wouldn't be opposed to it."

Tony's eyes widened but he didn't say anything. Instead he stayed quiet with the other three while the pastor scratched his head and let out a long breath.

"Okay, well, can I help you sort through your problems?" the pastor asked. "You guys are real distracting out here, you know?"

"I don't think you can help us," Val said in a defeated tone. "I don't think anyone can."

The pastor smiled. "Well, first of all, nothing is impossible for God. And second... You know I was in there writing a sermon about how the church is like one body and every member is a different body part. And even though the parts are different they all work together. But that can apply to friend groups, too. You are all parts of a whole, each of you working separately, but together for a common goal. Does that make sense?"

"Yeah," Tony said nodding. He glanced at Sam first, then Ana, and finally Val. "Yeah, it does."

The others quietly agreed and the pastor let out a relieved breath. "Okay, I don't know why I felt that would help. But if it means you'll stop arguing on my lawn, that's great. Now you four have a good night. I have a sermon to finish."

He turned and walked away from them while his words sank in. Four parts of one whole. Surely they could make this work.

# Chapter Twenty-Three

The four of them, now standing in a tight circle, looked around at each other. Sam and Tony locked eyes, while Ana lifted an eyebrow at Val and Val half nodded at her. Could they make this work? Absolutely. Would it be hard? Insanely so.

"What do we need to work on first?" Tony said.

"Your running technique," Ana said quickly. "Your pitching's gotten a lot better, but you still need to hit the bases somehow. While you do that, I'll read your story to Sam."

Tony pursed his lips. They'd all been in his book, in his story, in his head by now. He nodded wearily, but when Val offered to time him, he felt even more trepidation. He'd been working so hard at being a pitcher that he'd forgotten the other side of baseball. Still, he took off at a fast pace, making the church lawn his borrowed diamond. Hopefully the pastor wouldn't mind a little running.

Once Tony had gotten all the way around to the backside of the church, Sam cleared his throat and said, "I thought you were going to read to me."

"No," she said, her gaze shifting to the other side of the church as Tony emerged there. "He's amazing, isn't he?"

Sam glanced at Val whose eyebrows rose. "Uh…yes?" Sam said. "He sure is. Hey, what part are you going to read? The mushy bit with the romance or…?"

Ana finally ripped her gaze away from Tony. "No, I'm doing the part where Valentino finds the sword. But I really don't need to practice reading it. It'll be right there in front of me."

Val nudged Sam. "You could do the same. Or…did you actually memorize my speech?"

Sam lifted his chin. "Yeah, I know it."

Val crossed her arms. "Prove it."

"Incinerators," Sam started dramatically. "What are they and how can they help the world? As the name would suggest, incinerators incinerate. More specifically, they incinerate garbage, which we can all agree—" he paused to give a cheeky smile "—is causing a massive problem with overfilling landfills and clogging up oceans. Killing wildlife on both land and sea. We are quite literally swimming in our own trash!" Sam raised his arms like he was prepared to do a butterfly dive.

"Okay," Val said, taking his wrists and pulling them back down. "The extra embellishments aren't necessary."

Sam stared blankly at her. "Don't you…want to win your debate?"

"Of course. That's why the points I made are so strong."

"Okay, but you weren't just going to recite it, right?" He looked at Ana, who just shrugged. She had no idea what Val would have done had she not switched bodies with someone else. "You would have put some excitement into your voice, made some gestures with your hands? Anything?"

Val shook her head and gave Ana a look but again Ana had no idea how to save her from this. She was on Sam's side. Tony raced up to them, huffing and puffing.

"What are we doing?" he rasped out. "Why am I the only one doing things?"

"Sam's...saying my speech," Val said flatly. "Better than me apparently."

"No," Ana said gently. "He was just trying to make it exciting. You were given a terrible topic, it had nothing to do with your words."

"But I...I always do my debates like that."

Sam's face scrunched up. "Like what?"

Val took a deep breath and while letting it out repeated the first sentence for them. It was quick—like she wanted to get through it as quickly as possible—devoid of emotion, and monotonous enough that each word seemed to have equal importance. She finished the paragraph Sam had said for them but ended it quietly.

After, the others stared in a perplexed way, and Sam said slowly, "I can...do it like that if you really want."

"No, don't do that," Ana said quickly.

"Yeah, please don't," Tony said. "I get super nervous talking in front of people but even I wouldn't read a speech that plainly."

"Fine!" Val threw up her hands. "You can do it your way, Sam, since you're so naturally charismatic and charming and everyone loves you. You could win anyone over to your side. Go ahead."

"Val..." he said softly. He took her hands and held them firmly but gently. "I'm not naturally anything. But you are *so* smart and *so* good at things. If I had your talent, I could do whatever want."

She huffed. "You *should* be going out there and doing anything you want."

Sam shrugged. "Well, what I really want is to become a model. And...maybe one day show off my art. Who knows?"

She shook her head and looked at Ana, who nodded encouragingly.

"Hey," Sam said, "if it helps you could just do what you do for your speeches but with my pictures. It really fits the vibe. I once got turned down for a photoshoot because I was…" He cringed. "Too smiley."

"Really?"

"Seriously, it crushed him for weeks," Tony said.

Val couldn't help a sad chuckle. Sam's smile was the best thing about him and those people were wrong to try to snuff that out. "Alright, I'll try for a little stoicism. But really, anyone who doesn't want your smile is missing out."

Sam smiled shyly. And then they stared into each other's eyes until Ana cleared her throat and Tony nudged Sam. Realizing he was still holding Val's hands, Sam abruptly dropped them and wiped his own down the pencil skirt.

"Can I wear this tomorrow?" Sam said.

"Yes," Val answered confidently. "You dress way better than me."

He tilted his head, considering her. "That doesn't matter. I'm sorry I ever said that it did."

"It's fine, Sam." Val turned her head towards the other two, who had mysteriously gotten several feet away from them. "Are they slowly backing away from us?"

Giggling, Tony shouted, "Nope!" and he and Ana both turned and ran.

Sam frowned. "What's up with that?"

"I don't know." Val shook her head. "But she did tell me she likes him and that she has for a while so maybe she's not as unhappy about this as we are."

Sam laughed. "I'm not unhappy, Val. This is weird and inconvenient, and I'm sorry you're unhappy, but I'm not."

A soft smile touched her lips. "It could be worse, I guess. I could have ended up in the body of a guy with a really bad attitude. Or one who was into something terrible, like wrestling."

"Okay, I'm also really grateful you're not a wrestler. Ty convinced me to play football for a bit and that felt way too close to wrestling. Thank you for just being…you."

Feeling her face heating up from the compliment, she looked away. "Well…thank you for making me look like an amazing artist."

"You really like my art?"

She gave him a sharp look, wondering why he would sound so shy when he asked. "Yes? It's awesome!"

"Oh… Do you want to see what I was working on earlier?" Sam pulled out his phone. "I took pictures because I liked them so much but now I'm wondering if I'm actually as good as I think I am. I'm probably not."

She took the phone he held out—which was actually hers—and looked at the screen. There was the rough outline of two fantasy creatures, Valentino and Sparkle, their lips locked. Somehow, Sam had managed to include Valentino's protruding teeth in the mix, but it didn't look bad. Val liked it a lot, even with the absence of defined lines and colour. It was beautiful.

"I love this," she whispered. Feeling awkward for using the L-word, she smiled and joked, "I'm so glad you took this on my phone so I can keep it when I get my body back."

He smiled back at her but didn't know how to answer. He would lose this picture along with the phone—and likely Val—if and when they switched back. "What if you don't get it back, though? And get stuck being a dumb male model for the rest of your life?"

"You're not dumb, and I'd totally be happy to do that. If I could figure out how to actually pose."

"You'll be fine. Just follow the photographer's instructions." He looked past her to the sun hanging low in the sky. "I guess we should go. The pastor might come out and shoo us away."

"Can I come over and hear the whole speech?"

"Come over to who's house?"

She shrugged. "I guess it doesn't matter at this point."

*      *      *

After making their not-so-subtle retreat, Ana and Tony headed in the direction of Ana's house. They took their time, though, enjoying the sun as it lazily set on the horizon. At some point, Ana's hand had found Tony's and they had yet to let go of each other.

"I guess it wouldn't be terrible to be stuck like this," Ana said softly. "I could even finish your book for you!"

He smiled, knowing she was only half serious. "If we are stuck, I'm taking this body to the doctor, Ana."

"How'd I know you would say that?"

"I'm worried about you."

"Why?"

"Because, I—" He stopped to think. Ana would never have been able to describe her pain to him in a way he would have truly understood. Now that he'd felt it, things were different. "I care about you. No one should have to live with the kind of pain you have."

She smiled at him. "You're very sweet, Tony. It's one of the things I like best about you."

He shook his head, telling himself not to get impatient with her brushing him off. "Okay, you know what? I don't need your permission. This is *my* body now. I'll take myself to the doctor after the game."

"I won't stop you."

"Good."

They'd reached Ana's home. There were no cars in the driveway. Ana missed her family, and she knew if they didn't switch back, the only way to continue seeing them would be to stay *at least* friends with Tony.

Ana let herself in and as soon as she and Tony were inside, Abuela called out to her. Ana elbowed Tony and quietly said that Abuela was in the living room, and they should go say hi to her. Tony led the way and Abuela smiled when he popped his head in. Her smile grew when she saw Ana.

"¿Quien es?" Abuela said, while nodding her head at Ana. He wondered how many times Abuela would ask before remembering. If she ever would.

"That's Tony," he answered, almost effortlessly.

"Ohhh…" Abuela got up and patted Ana's cheeks while she pursed her lips to hold back laughter. "I *know* you."

"You do?" Ana asked in awe.

"Yes." Abuela nodded firmly. "Yes, I do. You're Ana's boyfriend!"

"That's right, I am," Ana said enthusiastically, mirth sparkling in her eyes.

Abuela reached out and patted Ana's cheek. "*Muy guapo.*"

And then with that, she turned and left without even talking to Tony, who she must have thought was her granddaughter. Ana chuckled as she took Tony by the wrist to lead him up to her bedroom.

"Hey," Tony whispered under his breath. "Why did you tell her that?"

"She has Alzheimer's," she answered with a shrug. "I doubt she'll remember by the time everyone else gets home. And besides…" She gazed into Tony's eyes as she pushed her bedroom door open. "If we're stuck like this, I have to have some excuse to see my family. Might as well pretend to be your boyfriend so I can have a meal with them every once in a while."

"Oh, Ana…" His eyes widened sympathetically. "We're not stuck, I promise. But when we get our bodies back, can I still come eat here sometimes? Your mom made something amazing last night and I would love to have that again."

"Of course," she said with an easy smile. "Anything you want."

"Anything?"

She nodded.

"I would love to see *you* play a game."

Ana's heart picked up speed. That was quite possibly the nicest thing any boy had ever said to her. She stuck her hand out towards him. "When we get back into our own bodies, you can watch *all* my games and I'll read your finished book."

He smiled brightly and put his hand in hers. "Deal."

As they shook hands, Tony briefly considered telling her what he really wanted to do if he got his body back was to kiss her again. For real. Maybe she'd actually go for that.

# Chapter Twenty-Four

Sam normally would not have gotten up too early on a Saturday. But knowing his best friend, Sam would have bet Val's mom's blazer that Tony was up and already pacing in his room. And if there was ever a time they needed each other it was now.

After dressing himself in something casual—for now, so he didn't get it messy—he ate a quick breakfast alone. It seemed the entire Davis family liked to sleep in. Well, except for Shadow. He faithfully lay next to Sam's chair, despite seemingly knowing that Sam wasn't Val. The two had gotten along quite nicely over the last couple of days and Sam knew if he got his body back, he would miss seeing Shadow.

Though, if he were honest, he'd say he would miss being part of a proper family. That made him feel a little guilty considering what a kind brother he had. But the truth remained. Sam liked feeling like he had a doting mom, an adoring dad, and two siblings who didn't have to pretend to be either one to him. Tony's family had filled a little of the void, too, but it still wasn't the same.

He was tempted to go back to sleep and just succumb to living out the rest of his life like that. But that wouldn't be fair to Val. And he had important things to do. Like make sure Tony at least looked pretty while butchering Ana's game.

When Sam got to Ana's house, he almost let himself in like he was used to doing at Tony's. Instead, he texted Tony. Tony, who had barely slept, answered within a few seconds and was promptly at the door.

"I can't do this," Tony said as soon as he'd swung the door open.

"Sure, you can," Sam said easily. "All you're doing is throwing a ball. And then a little heavy running. You'll be totally fine."

His eyes wide, Tony said plaintively, "I have to catch the balls sometimes, too!"

"Yeah…we probably should have told her you can't catch to save your life."

"I can't do this."

Sam just sighed, grabbed Tony's elbow and led him inside. They went up to Ana's room and Sam looked around for anything that resembled makeup and hair products. She had a small, modest supply. That would do. Sam got the hairbrush and turned to Tony.

"What are you doing?" Tony asked.

"Just let me help."

"Help with what?"

Rolling his eyes, he put his hands on Tony's shoulders and spun him around. "Trust me. I'm your best friend in the whole world, remember?"

"Yeah, but what are you doing?"

Sam poked around Ana's stuff and took a few things, including a special black tube. "Remember when you made me read *Peter Pan* in seventh grade?"

"Yes…"

"And in the book, everyone always says how all you need is faith, trust, and a little pixie dust?"

"Right…"

Sam held up the black tube. "This is your pixie dust."

Tony frowned, his whole face crinkling up. "What is that?"

"*Pixie dust.* Now hold still."

Tony did hold still…for all of five seconds. Sam was literally dusting something onto his face with a soft-bristle brush—makeup he assumed—and it made him want to sneeze. When he did sneeze, Sam scowled at him.

"What?" Tony said, before getting a mouthful of powder. "I can't help sneezing."

"Yeah, yeah."

"What is all that, though?" Tony pointed to the rest of the stuff.

"You know what it is," Sam said. "Don't worry, I'll bet anything it's all stuff you can sweat in. Plus, this eye black will help with any glare from the sun."

"Oh, good," Tony said sarcastically. "Wouldn't want the sun to get in my eyes and wreck my game."

Ignoring Tony's sarcasm, Sam said, "Exactly. And you're welcome."

Tony shut his mouth after that, choosing instead to be grateful that his best friend had stuck by him throughout this entire incredibly awkward situation. Granted, Sam was in the same position. But Tony knew, without a shadow of a doubt, that he would have acted the same way were he not in Val's body right now.

"Thank you," Tony said when it seemed Sam was finally finished applying layers of protective creams and balms and even something over his eyes. "I don't know how it'll help me play better but thank you anyway."

Sam smiled and held up the eye black, the last part of the look. "This actually *will* help. Plus, you'll look super cool."

"Great," Tony said less than enthusiastically.

"You're gonna be fine." Sam swiped two thick black lines under Tony's eyes and then stepped away. "Perfect. I can't wait to watch you play. Your one and only sports gig! How exciting."

"I hope I don't screw it up."

"You won't." Sam stopped to smile. "And honestly, I'm glad Ana's doing your reading. I know you would have just skipped out on it."

Tony laughed. "You know me too well."

"Yes, I do."

When that was all done, Tony got into Ana's baseball gear. There were a lot of pieces, but once again, Sam was there to help. And so was the internet, because even Sam didn't know what some of this stuff was for. The chest protector was a new one, but they figured out how to get it on.

After he was dressed, Tony sent Sam to wait for him at the park. Then he went in search of Ana's mother, who was in the kitchen cooking. Tony took a big whiff, a smile growing on his face. It wouldn't be so bad to wake up to that smell for the rest of his life.

"Mami?"

Señora Dellagusta whirled around, a battered spatula in her hand. "Oh, Ana. You're already dressed."

"Yup," he said gesturing to himself.

Ana's mom pointed to the table where there were already eggs and bacon on large platters and orange juice in a glass pitcher. He sat and helped himself while she continued working on whatever she was making. The food was delicious but he had other things on his mind.

Gathering up his courage—and hoping Ana wouldn't hate him—he said, "Mami...I think I need to see the doctor."

"About what?" she said without even turning to him.

"It's...it's my period. It's too painful."

Mami looked at him, soft sympathy in her eyes. "It's gotten that bad?" Tony just nodded, because he didn't know how bad it was before. "Okay, mija. We'll call on Monday."

He let out a relieved breath. "Thank you." If nothing else, at least maybe he wouldn't have to be in so much pain forever.

*     *     *

Ana had all but forgotten about that part of her life. She had a new life now, it seemed. But she wasn't worried about the reading. In fact, she'd practiced speaking out loud last night, even taking a few tips from the "erroneous" way Sam had recited Val's speech. But she did feel a little guilty that she'd lied to Tony about what part she would read. The sword was great and all, but nothing compared to that scene where Valentino and Sparkle nearly kill each other before reluctantly agreeing to work together.

The fact that she'd accidentally added a kiss into the mix made the scene that much better. Even Tony had admitted it, but she knew he would never have the guts to *read* that out loud. She would just have to do it for him.

Now to see what kind of nerdy clothes he had in his closet. She couldn't very well wear jeans and a t-shirt. Especially not since she wanted to stop by her game first. She had just enough time for the first inning, at least.

There was a suit in the closet, Ana discovered. A soft grey one with properly tailored pants and a jacket. It was overkill. She knew it. But when she put it on with a light blue dress shirt and looked in the mirror in the bathroom, her heart skipped a beat. Tony could wear this suit every day to school and he'd have most of the girls eating out of his hand.

Ana looked at her hands. She didn't want any of the girls, but she did want to make a good impression today for Tony's sake.

Tony had a couple of ties and Ana chose a paisley blue and white one. But she had no idea how to tie it and no inclination to learn. She took the tie to the kitchen where she found Maddy making a cup of tea. Ana cleared her throat and Maddy turned around, her eyebrows immediately shooting up to her hairline.

As they lowered, she came closer and whispered, "Tony?"

Ana smiled slyly. "Not yet. But I'm glad to know I chose something he'd wear."

Maddy shook her head, chuckling. "I don't know if he'd pick it on his own, but Sam might make him wear that. You look great."

"Thanks. Any idea how to tie this?" Ana held up the tie.

"No, but Mom does." Maddy waved her hand loosely towards the den. "And I'm sure she'll *love* seeing you in that."

"Thanks."

Ana headed towards the den, feeling awkward in Tony's body and his suit. Of course, it had been awkward the entire week. But she hadn't had to ask anyone to help her get dressed in a long time. Even when she got ready for her games, she did all her equipment herself. She didn't need anyone.

But then when Mrs. Cleaver smiled so adoringly at her and immediately reached for the tie, Ana lost the battle to remain impartial. Tony's family wasn't the worst one to be unwittingly adopted into.

"You look *so* handsome, Anthony," Mrs. Cleaver said as she deftly tied the tie around Ana's neck. "And I'm so proud you're doing this today. Everyone should know how talented you are."

"You know what?" Ana smiled. "You're right. They should know."

Mrs. Cleaver chuckled. "There's that confidence. It hasn't always been there. I'm sure Sam had a lot to do with it. But there's…something else. Something different about you."

"Oh, yeah?" Ana said, trying her best to keep her voice even so she wouldn't give herself away.

"Yeah," Mrs. Cleaver said softly as she patted down the knot she'd made. "You're just becoming a man. And someday you'll be gone, and some other woman will tie your ties."

She'd gotten a little teary-eyed and Ana swallowed hard. She might be stuck being Mrs. Cleaver's baby for the rest of her life. It wasn't the worst fate, but if it were true, she had to choose the right thing to say.

She settled on, "If it helps, I can marry a girl who *can't* tie a tie."

Mrs. Cleaver laughed delightedly and kissed Ana's cheek. "That helps, yes."

Ana looked down at the tie, happy she'd gone through the trouble. "I have to go somewhere really quick. I'll see everyone at the community centre."

"Oh!" Mrs. Cleaver looked surprised, but she never dropped her smile. "Sure, sweetheart. As long as this isn't a ruse to get out of doing your reading."

"I would never," Ana said honestly. "I'll see you soon."

The baseball diamond wasn't too far from Tony's house. It made Ana wonder if he'd ever walked past one of her games. Regardless, she was here to see him. The teams were just taking their positions, so Ana scanned the bleachers for a good spot to sit. Her family was here. Davide and Papi were deep in discussion, while Mami was holding hands with Abuela. There was an empty spot next to Davide, but it would be weird for her to sit there.

A frantically waving hand caught her eye, and it took her a moment to realize Sam was waving her down. She smiled and rushed over to him. It was nice to have a friend in the stands. She was so overwhelmed that she hugged him as soon as she'd sat next to him.

"What'd I miss?" she asked.

"Just the warm-ups," he answered. "Tony did a couple of pitches, and he didn't look bad."

"Good, good."

"And speaking of not looking bad…" Sam looked her up and down with a cheeky grin. "I think I've only ever seen Tony wear that suit to a funeral."

"Well, he looks good, so…"

"Uh huh."

"Shh, I'm watching the game."

Tony had no idea Ana had popped by to catch the start of the game. He was too busy trying to keep his nervous stomach from tossing the delicious breakfast Mami had made for him. She'd repeated many times about keeping his energy up, how his period had likely drained a lot from him, and how he would need to get through "all nine innings and no more," as she didn't want to have to sit through overtime.

Tony didn't even know if his throwing arm would last through at least half the game. But he would try his best. Unfortunately, the visiting team got to bat first, which meant it was do or die for him. Right now.

He went up to the pitcher's mound and waited for Sarah to crouch down, her catcher's helmet lowered over her face. Once the batter was in position, Tony tossed his ball…straight to the bat. A crack caused the ball the fly above and past Tony's head, and their opponent got to first base before the ball dropped too far away from their outfielder to catch it. Shaking her head in disappointment, Ariel picked it up and threw it to Tony.

He caught it—just barely—and took a deep breath. Great. He'd let the very first batter get to first base.

"Come on, Tony," he mumbled to himself.

He clutched the ball, willing it to be his best friend so he could get through this. As the next batter took her position, Sarah signaled to him. He was pretty sure she was asking for a curve ball. He didn't think he had enough control to make any of the throws just right.

Ana had taught him there were different ways to grip the ball in order to make the throws different. Would he remember them all? No. But would he try his hardest to not let her team down? Absolutely.

Making his best educated guess, he lobbed the ball but not too hard so it would go slower and therefore make the kind of arch he was hoping for. The batter swung—far too early—and Sarah caught the ball gleefully. At least, it seemed gleeful to Tony. He was happy about that. *And* he managed two more no-hitters to strike this batter out. Maybe this wouldn't end terribly.

# Chapter Twenty-Five

Val had given herself plenty of time to get ready for the local author's reading at the community centre. But when it came time to get dressed, she wasn't sure what to even wear. Val had always thought of Sam's style as being so oddly out there that she'd never really understood it. Sometimes it was button-down shirts with a combo of floral and stripes. Sometimes it was pink board shorts and a plain tank top. And other times it was a graphic tee with a cartoon hamburger on it.

She still didn't quite get it, but one thing was for sure—Sam *always* looked good. He knew what worked and she assumed she could wear anything in his closet and it would be fine. He'd already shown her the special clothes he was taking to his photoshoot, so she left those alone and chose something else.

A pair of light-wash jeans and an oversized knit cardigan with a striped shirt underneath would do just fine. It was comfortable enough—since she'd gotten used to the tightness of his pants—and as she'd predicted, she looked great. She just hoped she didn't overshadow Ana.

Of course, she felt that way before she got to the community centre and actually saw Ana, dressed like she was ready for either church or a date. She had to wonder who Ana was trying to impress. Ana had already admitted that she liked Tony and it wasn't like Tony would care if he looked good in his own clothes. Or maybe he would?

Val shook her head. It didn't matter. They could worry about the logistics later. After today.

Hall C3 had been reserved for the local author's reading and it was already decently full when Val walked in. She scanned the crowd and saw Ana sitting up near the front, sandwiched between Tony's sisters. Ana turned in her seat to look around and locked eyes with Val. She stood and waved with an enthusiastic smile and Val couldn't help smiling back. Ana was too cool for taking this whole thing in stride.

Ana came towards Val and they met in the aisle. Ana clasped Val's elbows and Val put her hands on Ana's forearms.

"Look at *you*," Val said. "Swanky."

"Yeah, but you always look good."

"Like this, sure."

Ana laughed. "Come sit with the family. I'm pretty sure they're expecting that."

"Of course."

Val went up to the row of seats again and Tony's parents and sisters greeted her affectionately. She'd never had a friend whose family treated her like family and it was…nice. Like nice enough that she could get used to that if she never got her own life back.

They had to sit through an introduction and two other authors before Tony was even mentioned. Val was impressed that other than the tapping of Ana's foot on the floor, she seemed cool as a cucumber. Val was nervous just thinking about her upcoming photoshoot.

Ana, if she were honest, had never done public speaking before and didn't actually know what to expect. She'd been mulling over her chosen excerpt in her head when the MC announced Anthony Cleaver. And then announced his name again. Val elbowed Ana and whispered that that was *her.*

"Ah, there he is," the MC said as Ana made her way to the makeshift stage. "Perfect. Here he is, our youngest writer. Anthony, why don't you tell us a little about yourself and what you're writing and then you can read us your excerpt?"

"Oh, um…" Ana hadn't come prepared to talk about Tony. She liked him plenty but didn't know how he would introduce himself. Come to think of it, Tony would talk down about himself. She wasn't going to, though. She took the mic and said, "Hi, I'm Anthony. That's my family down there. And my best friend." Val gave her a smile and nodded. "I'm a fantasy writer. I love worldbuilding but I love even more my…quirky characters." That was a phrase Tony would use. "They're all mythical creatures. My main character is an orc named Valentino. And he's sort of frenemies with this fairy named Sparkle. And, well, the scene I have features them."

She took a deep breath and glanced at Val, who had taken out her phone to…record her? Oh no, when Tony found out she had switched the scene, he wouldn't be happy. But she would have to deal with that later. She knew this was the right choice. Romance just sold better than fighting.

The words on Ana's phone danced in front of her but she consciously forced herself to slow down. This wasn't that hard. There weren't even that many people and it wasn't even her book. This was fine.

As confidently as she could, she read the part that set up the scene. Valentino had been sneaking around an enemy's base in the dead of night, using only the moonlight as his guide. Just because he was an orc didn't mean he had to be clumsy or loud, and he tiptoed towards a tent that hopefully held what he was looking for.

However, when he flipped back the curtain, the only thing waiting for him was his sometimes-friend, sometimes-foe Sparkle. She had her back turned to him, but he didn't need to see her face to know. He'd recognize her anywhere, hood and all. Ana stopped reading for a moment to explain that by this point, Sparkle had already made a few appearances in the book and while she and Valentino didn't outright hate each other, she usually tried her best to foil his plans.

Sparkle held a glistening object up for inspection. Though it looked like a solid rock, it pulsed with living, vibrant energy. The heart of the dragon, which belonged *to* the dragon. Valentino had been sent to retrieve it and he wasn't going to fail his mission now.

Silently, he crept towards her and when he'd almost got to her, he reached out towards her. But she spun around and knocked his hand away. "Did you think your sneaking could disguise your awful breath?" she whispered indignantly.

He couldn't answer, for the rage that blinded him when he saw her trying to take his prize overwhelmed him. As quick as a snake lunging for its prey, Valentino grabbed the front of Sparkle's neck. He pulled her closer as her cheeks flushed a deep crimson.

"Why can't you ever stay out of my way?" he growled.

"Can't..." she squeaked out. "Can't...stop. Won't." She flicked the blade of her switch, tempted to plunge it straight into his heart if he didn't let her go.

He licked his lips as they turned down into an even bigger frown. His grip loosened, just enough for her to take in a deep breath. "Give me what I want."

She had the dragon's heart in one hand and her blade in the other, but Valentino ignored them both. Instead, he pulled her to himself and kissed her...for at least half a second before Sparkle freed herself enough to slap his cheek. She left a deep green mark on his face in the shape of her hand.

Ana paused for a moment as the audience chuckled. There wasn't a lot of humour in Tony's book, and she hoped he wouldn't mind that this bit was intentional. She thought it was funny that Sparkle would react like that to a surprise kiss.

Valentino barely budged, though he did move his hand to the back of her neck. Her lips, softening in the dim light of the dragon's heart, almost showed a smile as she allowed him to come closer again. As his forked tongue touched hers, she put her switch away, but still refused to let the heart go to him. At least, not the *dragon's* heart.

He pulled back enough to say, "So, we'll take it together, then?"

It was a trick. She was sure of it. But that didn't stop her from saying yes. "I'll carry the heart. You can…kill all the things."

"Agreed," he said gruffly, as if his lips hadn't been softly pressed against hers a moment ago.

As soon as they left the tent, Sparkle took to the sky, her wings beating powerfully but silently in the air. All Valentino could do was smile, shake his head, and sprint to keep up.

Ana stopped there, but when there was no response, she smiled and said, "That's it." The audience applauded for her, appreciatively if she weren't mistaken.

The MC came back and asked, "Do they end up together?"

"I couldn't say," Ana answered honestly, knowing it would just come off as cheeky.

The MC chuckled. "Any other comments or questions?"

A bunch of hands went up and Ana had to stifle her gasp. Tony was a talented writer, but she hadn't expected so many people to have something to say about the scene. Some of them just wanted to say that they liked it. Others asked her questions about the book that she couldn't possibly answer, though she did try to give vaguely enthusiastic answers.

One young woman did put up her hand to explain how a fairy and orc pairing would never work due to the obvious differences in their reproductive organs. Ana had no idea what kind of fantasy fiction she'd been reading, but she was in no position to address that.

Instead, with her face flaming brightly, she leaned towards the mic and said, "My parents are in the audience."

"Oh, sorry," the questioner mumbled.

That was when the MC decided to cut off Ana's question and answer period. He motioned to the chairs and said, "Thank you so much, Anthony, we look forward to seeing the finished product."

Ana smiled amid more applause as she left the stage. It wasn't even her book and it filled her with warmth to think of seeing it finished, bound nicely with a cover Sam had designed. What a sight that would be.

As she approached Tony's family, she could barely make contact with his sisters, whose eyebrows had inched up their foreheads. She'd probably ruined the innocent image they had of their little brother. But Val looked impressed, mirthful even as Ana sat next to her.

"I can't believe you read that scene," Val whispered while the MC moved onto the next author.

"I know, he's gonna kill me," Ana said. "Don't show him that video."

Val just giggled…as much as Sam's voice could giggle. "Do we have to sit through many more of these or are we making a run for it?"

"No, we should sit," Ana answered.

198

And she did, but it was with a lot of impatience. She was still hoping she could catch some more of her own game before it ended. Thankfully, there were only three other authors, though one of them read five whole chapters of her book. And she would have read more if the MC hadn't cut her off, citing the ending of the booked time in that room.

Finally, Ana was free… But not from the compliments that came flooding to her from Tony's family and some other people who eagerly wanted to chat.

Ana sent a desperate look Val's way, who said, "Oh, Tony, remember that thing we gotta get to? Let's go get to it."

"*Right.* The thing. Mom, Dad, see you later." Ana sent another look Maddy's way, hoping Maddy would cover for her.

"A thing." Maddy chuckled and turned to her family, effectively cutting them off from Ana and Val. "Sounds like he wants to see a *girl.* Bye, Tony. Bye, Sam. Enjoy your double date."

Ana rushed away without another word and Val kept up with her. Ana pulled the jacket off and draped it over her arm before loosening the tie. She'd grown too hot and uncomfortable in it, and she wanted the freedom to basically run back to the baseball field.

Val wasn't much of a runner, but she felt Ana's urgency and they made good time. In fact, Ana was pleased the game was still going when they got there.

She slid into the seat next to Sam and Val sat next to her. Urgently, Ana asked, "Okay, what did I miss?"

"It's the bottom of the ninth," Sam said without even taking his eyes off the field. "We're down by one point, we've got two on base, and, uh…you're up to bat."

"Oh." Ana's heart suddenly fluttered nervously. She knew what she would do in this situation. She'd hit any ball that even remotely looked like it would make it infield. But one week hadn't been enough to teach Tony every nuance of the game. She just had to hope he'd take his best shot.

"He hasn't been doing too badly," Sam said softly. "He did get replaced as pitcher in the sixth, but that seemed like a normal call. His batting average is surprisingly good considering he's, well, Tony."

"Hmm…"

The first pitch thrown his way was a strike. Tony swung far too late, and Ana wasn't sure she believed Sam about his batting average. The second pitch, however, was a ball—a bad mistake by the other pitcher. Ana started tapping her leg.

The third pitch—oh, that one was *just* right. A little too good. Tony hit it for all his worth. The ball cracked against the bat and went soaring through the air in a perfect arc. For a second, Tony just watched it as though stunned.

"Oh no, oh no, oh no," Ana mumbled into her balled up hands.

"What's wrong?" Val asked. "That's an awesome hit."

"Yeah, but it's easy to—" The ball flew towards one of the outfielders' gloves. "Catch."

But the ball didn't stay in the glove as the other player accidentally dropped it. The crowd roared and it took Tony another moment to realize what had happened. He began running as his teammates rounded the bases.

First base was easy for him as the other team was still trying to get their ball infield. Second base was a little more difficult as he had to scoot around another player waiting to catch the ball and tag him. By then, his two teammates had made it home and that was the game.

But he didn't want to just stop there. Not when their opponents were still actively trying to get him out and his team was chanting Ana's name over and over. So, he raced to third as the ball blew over his head. It didn't make it there on time and, after quickly tapping the base, he sprinted to home. At the very last second, he threw himself to the ground, taking a dive and sliding with his left foot out in front of him. His foot touched the base a second before the other player with the ball did. The umpire called it a home run and Tony merely rolled over wearily.

His entire team rose to their feet, cheering and clapping, and rushed towards him. Sarah and April pulled him up and the rest of them attempted to smother him with hugs. He laughed. It felt good to have won the game and gotten so many runs from someone else's mistake. But at the same time, he wished Ana could be there. Not to see him, but to gloat over the other team.

He looked up into the stands, past her family who was coming towards him and past the other audience members who were leaving. There were Sam, Val, and Ana. Ana waved and he waved back. She looked happy…but also not happy. This was her victory and he'd stolen it.

# Chapter Twenty-Six

Sam and Val didn't have time to wait for Tony to tell him how amazing he was. They both needed to change their clothes and get places. It was unfortunate especially for Sam because he was so excited for Tony's only sporting event.

But Sam wanted to go back to get Val's mom's awesome blazer and do Val's makeup just perfect. He would never admit that he'd spent a chunk of last evening watching videos online to help him figure out the best way to make Val even more gorgeous than she already was. And he knew she would say it didn't matter, that the debate was about what came out of her brain. But he still wanted to dress up.

The truth was, that if Val were honest, she'd say the eyeliner and simple foundation Sam had asked her to wear brought out his already lovely features. And she knew that if there was ever a time to be vain about how she looked, it was while she was in the body of a model going to a gig. She'd learned to accept this, even though she wasn't sure she could do it forever. But she would figure that out later.

For now, she was carefully packing up the clothes she needed when Ana burst into Sam's bedroom.

Ana flashed her gaze at him. "Are you almost ready? Ty looks super nervous and he's jangling his keys a lot."

"Oh." Val closed up the small suitcase. Of course Ty was nervous. Someone else was taking his brother's place at an important job. "I'm ready. Let's go."

As soon as she walked out into the living room, he said, "There you are," in a half exasperated, half relieved voice. "Let's go. I don't want you to be late and I got stuff to do. Are you going, too, Tony?"

"Yes," Ana said eagerly. "I would never abandon Sam."

Ty gave her a tight smile. "You never have."

Val *almost* laughed out loud. Ty knew she wasn't Sam, but he had no idea that Tony wasn't Tony. But Ana had embodied him so perfectly that Ty had no idea. Or maybe Ty really was in too much of a hurry to figure it out. Either way, Val hurried along with the other two to Ty's car in the parking lot.

It was a good ten-minute drive to the studio and when Ty parked, he turned to Val with a serious look in his eye. "You good?"

Val tried to channel Sam's confidence when she nodded. "Yeah. I got this."

"Okay. Just follow the photographer's instructions. Everything will be fine."

"Of course it will." Val smiled. "Thank you."

"Mmhmm. I'll be back in two hours. Bye."

He was terse but Val couldn't blame him. It wasn't his fault that Val was here instead of Sam. But Val couldn't think of that right now. She had a job to do.

She went into the studio and was immediately greeted by a receptionist who brusquely said, "Name?"

"Va—" Val cleared her throat. "Samuel Dekker."

"Ah, yes," the woman said. "Male model three. Go down that hall to your left to the second door. Hair and makeup will meet you there, and the photographer will chat with you after that."

Val touched her hair, which she'd attempted to style nicely. How could hair and makeup possibly improve on *Sam,* of all people? She didn't get a chance to ask or comment when the woman continued.

"Your friend can go with you, but he'll have to stay out of the way."

"Thanks," Val said woodenly.

Ana linked arms with her and turned her in the right direction. With a smile, she said quietly, "Come on. If nothing else, this seems like it'll be a lot of fun, right? Try to enjoy it."

"Yeah. Sure."

But Val was more nervous than she'd been for anything else. She could do all the public speaking in the world, but feeling like she was on display— even if in someone else's body—made her entirely uncomfortable. Sam had made it sound easy, but he liked to be seen. She didn't.

Then again, with a face like his, it probably *was* easy. Forcing herself to relax, she went into the room she'd been directed to. Two middle-aged women looked over at her so she introduced herself.

The one holding a makeup brush looked all over Val's face before saying, "Yeah, I can work with that."

Val gave Ana a nervous look, but Ana bit her lip like she was holding back a chuckle. Val wanted to roll her eyes, but the makeup artist was already getting out more makeup to put on her. This felt like it was going to be a very long two hours.

*    *    *

Sam had gone back to Val's house, and for the first time in a long time, nerves ate away at him. He remembered the last time he'd gotten that nervous. It was two and a half years ago when he'd reluctantly packed up what he could in two suitcases while avoiding his father. When everything he owned was more or less ready to go, he went into the den where his father sat half asleep with a beer bottle in his hand.

Sam had no idea how much his father had drunk that night. Sometimes he drank enough to take the edge off. Sometimes it was enough to put the edge back on and that was when Sam worried the most. It seemed silly now, but at the time Sam, a fresh-faced 14-year-old, had a stomach boiling over with anticipation and anxiousness.

"Dad." When his dad had barely roused, Sam repeated the word. Finally, his dad had looked up, his eyes glassy. It had broken Sam's heart, but Ty had convinced him that nothing Sam could do would change their dad. "I'm leaving."

"Okay."

That one word broke Sam's heart even more. "No, Dad. I'm *leaving* leaving. I'm moving in with Ty."

"And I said *okay*," his dad had answered. He almost looked ready to get out of his seat, so Sam backed out of the room without another word.

He'd been afraid at the time that his dad might follow and do something to try to keep him there. Beg, beat... It didn't matter. Sam had been afraid. But Ty had shown up 30 seconds later and taken him away from that life and they hadn't seen their dad since.

Sam's grades and quality of life had vastly improved since then and he was happy now. He was confident at school and had a good outlook on life. But this feeling inside him as he got dressed in the nice outfit he'd picked out for Val's debate reminded him of that time. He didn't like that.

He went down into the living room and found Mrs. Davis peacefully drinking some tea. She looked up and smiled. "Wow, honey, you look so cute."

Sam put a hand against his fluttering stomach and frowned. "I don't feel so good."

Mrs. Davis's smile softened as she rose and came over. She put her arm around his shoulders and said, "You always get so nervous. And for nothing! You're going to be great. Want me to do your hair?"

"Yes, please," he said. He'd take any help he could get.

Mrs. Davis had him sit in a chair in the kitchen. She said she had the time for a couple of simple braids to "jazz up" a ponytail but that was it. Sam was more than happy with that. If it was out of his face, he didn't care what she did.

At least that was what he thought before she started tugging on his hair, creating a pin prickle sensation on his scalp. He kept his mouth clamped shut and breathed through it. Beauty was pain after all. The old adage was confirmed when she held her small mirror in front of him. Mrs. Davis clearly knew how to work with Val's hair and the shape of her face. Sam's eyes widened. "Wow, I'm so beautiful."

Laughing delightedly, Mrs. Davis set the mirror down and put her hands on either side of his face. "I've been telling you all your life. But I know you prefer people to think of you as smart and philosophical."

"Yeah, well—" He shrugged. "I think I can be all of it."

"You can." Mrs. Davis patted his cheeks gently and let go. "You all ready now?"

"You know what?" He smiled and patted his ponytail. "Now that I look amazing, I really am."

Mrs. Davis laughed again and then called to the rest of the family to get ready. Harrison and Juliette hadn't bothered to dress up for the occasion, but when Juliette saw Sam, she said was going to change "very quickly." Mrs. Davis gave her 30 seconds and she emerged in 45, wearing a pretty dress and white sneakers.

"Okay, *now* we're ready," Juliette said as she linked arms with Sam and started guiding him out to the family van. "It's about time you took my advice. People just listen better when you look better, you know?"

Sam couldn't have put it in better words. But at the same time, Val was worth listening to no matter what she looked like. "It never should matter, but maybe you're right. People listen with their eyes, too."

"Exactly."

On the short drive to the school, Sam recited Val's speech over and over in his head. The nerves he'd felt earlier were still there, but they weren't quite so intense. However, when he saw Tony waiting for him outside the front doors, the rest disappeared. How he wished he could express how grateful he was for Tony's constant companionship. He would have to save that for later, though, when Val's family wasn't there watching.

There were several people competing in the debate today, but there were no repeat arguments. Val had explained all of this. Only two people were given the incinerator debate, one person con and one person pro. She'd started telling him about the other debates and how much better they were but Sam had cut her off. He only needed to know what to do and when. He would go up with his opponent—who was unfortunately the very haughty Daniel Gillespie—and a coin toss would determine who got to present first.

Sam lost the coin toss and had to stand next to Daniel while he gave a very impassioned speech about air pollutants and toxins and the ozone. Sam didn't care much for either side or the debate itself. But it did irk him the way Daniel kept smirking in his direction and giving him side eye. Val deserved better, and Sam was glad he'd turned down a date with Daniel.

"In the end—" Daniel paused to once again give Sam a snotty look "—wouldn't you prefer *not* breathing in toxic gases? Let the air remain pure so it can heal the Earth. Thank you."

While the audience politely applauded, Sam got up to the podium. He could feel Daniel staring at him as they passed each other, but he wouldn't give him the satisfaction of staring back.

Sam could see now how annoying it could be to hear someone else give such an emotional-sounding speech to bring the audience on their side. But on the other hand, wasn't that what debate was all about? Convincing people to take your side using whatever means necessary?

Taking a deep breath to centre himself, he looked out at the audience and locked eyes with Tony. Then, he began to recite the speech Val had so carefully written. He made sure to hit all the relevant points: how safe incineration was, how it was a good alternative to landfill and could even be used for fuel, how any perceived cons were far outweighed by the pros.

"You see, while some people, like my opponent—" Sam couldn't help adding, though he still refused to look at Daniel "—may be comfortable literally living in and swimming in trash, there are others who aren't. Like the sea turtles. Dolphins. Raccoons, pigeons, squirrels. We've grown so accustomed to the philanthropy of *saving the whales* that we hadn't stopped to think that we should be saving *all of us*. There are so many things that can be safely burned and disposed of that every city on Earth should have an incineration plant." He smiled. "Maybe even two."

Val hadn't written that part, but Sam liked it as a conclusion. He grabbed the flaps of his jacket and gave a little bow as the audience applauded for him. It was hard to tell, but it seemed like they liked him better than Daniel. However, only the judges could decide whose was the best.

Sam forced his body to relax while he watched the judges speak quietly to one another. He could feel Daniel's eyes on him, but he ignored him. He was here for Val's sake and wouldn't start something when he knew she wouldn't either.

"Valerie Davis."

Sam shot right up when the centre judge called for him. "Yes?"

The judge smiled. "That was a wonderful speech. Congratulations. You won."

"Yay!" Sam couldn't help exclaiming.

As they stepped off the stage together, Daniel came closer and practically whispered in his ear. "That was a really good speech. I mean, for *you*. I can't help it. I still want to go out with you."

Sam finally looked at him, his face twisted in disgust. But it softened when he saw how serious Daniel was. And why wouldn't he want to go out with Val? She was awesome. "I appreciate that, but no thank you. Let's keep this…professional between us."

"Whatever, Davis, you freak."

Daniel turned and stalked away, and Sam didn't feel the least bit bad about turning him down. If Val was ever interested in Daniel, Sam had made sure to quash that. But in his mind, he'd done Val a favour. She wasn't a freak. She was amazing and smart and talented. Sam wouldn't be setting her up on any dates while in her body. In fact, he couldn't think of anyone who was even remotely good enough for her. And he would keep it that way.

# Chapter Twenty-Seven

Val thought two hours' worth of taking pictures would be torture. No one needed to spend that much time doing that with her. Then again, she was pretending to be Sam. And the camera *loved* Sam. So did the photographer.

After every setup and shot, Gill would hold out his camera and wave impatiently at Val to come over and look at the raw shots he'd taken. He gushed over her and how much he liked the way she posed for him. And Val had to admit the raw pictures, even on the tiny little camera screen, were amazing.

She also admitted—inwardly, to herself—that she was having fun. Each shot took a few minutes to set up and Gill wanted something different every time. Val got to pretend to be a prep student at a prestigious school, a skater punk with an attitude, and even a jailbird with no remorse. She hadn't the slightest idea what the purpose of these pictures was, but the dopamine hit that came every time she got to do new poses felt good. A little too good.

"Okay, for our last pose—"

The last one? That couldn't be right. How had two hours nearly flown by?

Gill had Val put on the white collared shirt with billowing sleeves and the black slacks. For once, Sam's pants weren't super tight. And when Val looked at herself in the mirror before stepping out from the change screen, she realized this was his best look. Or *hers* if she was stuck like this.

"Oh, that's wonderful," Gill said when she came out. "Okay, I want this to be very romantic. I know, boys don't like romance. But the camera does, and Gill does."

Val chuckled and met Ana's eyes across the room. She wasn't a boy, but she also didn't think much about romance. At least, not usually. Gill asked her to smile for the first time and she took her chance to give him a big one.

He frowned. "Not like *that*. Smile like you're thinking of your school crush, please."

"Oh."

Val didn't have a— The thought of Sam dressed in her mom's blazer just so he could make an impression at her debate meet filled her head. Blood rushed to her face and a smile did touch her lips right before the flash went off.

"Oh, that's perfect," Gill cooed. "Whoever she is is very lucky."

Val laughed at that because she couldn't help it. Gill had no idea. The flash went off again and Gill thanked her for the extra smile then waved her over. Val and Ana both went to look and when she saw the picture, Val's breath caught in her throat. She hadn't been lying when she said Sam's smile was his best feature and anyone should want to photograph it.

"Oh, wow, I would frame that," Ana said.

Val laughed. She would, too. If she were the type to keep a picture of Sam in her bedroom right next to her bed so she could see him before she went to sleep every night. Obviously, she wouldn't do that because that was crazy.

"Thank you so much, Samuel," Gill said as he shut off the camera. "I'll send some preliminary pictures in a week, okay? Now go, I have more clients."

"Thank you," Val said quietly.

She gathered her things and left with Ana at her side. Ty was already waiting in the parking lot and when he asked how everything went, Ana immediately piped up and said how awesome "Sam" had done.

Once they were home, Ana and Val went into Sam's bedroom. Val stripped off the fancy modeling clothes and changed into regular ones. She even put the others away, hanging them nicely so they wouldn't get ruined. All without saying a word.

"Are you okay?" Ana asked. "That was fun, right?"

"Yeah," Val answered honestly. "It kind of was."

"Then what's wrong?"

"Well… My debate meet is over by now. We did all the things. So why are we still like…this?" She gestured down at Sam's body.

"Oh. Good point. I guess I got used to it." Ana pulled out her phone. "Let's meet up with the guys."

"Good call."

It was with some modicum of relief that they all met that evening in front of the church once again. They'd made it through their harrowing Saturday and come out on the other side. Tony checked the window of the pastor's office, but it was dark in there. No one would come out and offer them advice tonight. Which was a shame, considering they were still stuck in each other's bodies.

"How did the debate meet go?" Val asked.

"We won!" Sam said happily. "And then Daniel asked you out and I told him I wanted to…*remain professional.*"

Val laughed out loud. "That's exactly how I would have said 'never in a thousand years.'"

Sam smiled, his dark eyes twinkling. "How was the photoshoot?"

"It was okay."

"She had *so* much fun," Ana said, jostling Val's arm. "You could totally tell. And the photographer loved her. Like he loved all her poses and thought her outfits looked great and it was just—"

"Ana," Tony said quietly. He jutted his chin towards Sam, whose downcast eyes were turned away.

"Oh, Sam." Val put her hand lightly on his arm. "I'm so sorry you missed it."

He shrugged and then gave her a tight smile. "I'm glad it was you. Tony would have made a mess of it."

"He's not wrong," Tony said. "But speaking of Tony, how was my reading?"

"Great, nothing to worry about," Ana said.

"I have a recording if you want to see it," Val said with a saucy smirk as she reached for her phone.

"That's not necessary," Ana said quickly, swatting at Val's hand. "Really. Everything was perfectly fine."

"Ana..." Tony put his hands on his hips and tried to look menacing, which was surprisingly not that difficult since he still had smudges of eye black under his eyes. "What happened?"

"Nothing," she said lightly. "Just, I...I chose a different scene. That's all."

His mouth slackened. "Don't tell me you read that kissing scene in front of my parents."

His cheeks flushed red. "I won't tell you that."

He sighed but Sam just giggled. Then they fell silent as the sun began to set on them once again. Tony touched Ana's jacket while she shoved her hands into the back pockets of his suit pants. Sam readjusted the flaps of Val's mom's blazer and Val ruined Sam's nice hairdo by shoving her fingers through it.

"What now?" Ana asked in a dejected tone.

Val shook her head and Tony mumbled something. Sam glanced around at his three friends and smiled, despite their strange dilemma.

"Hey, this isn't the worst thing in the world, right?" Sam said. "We could be stuck with way worse people. At least we're friends…right?"

Tony gave him a half smile. "And we're way hotter this way, Sunny."

Sam laughed while Val rolled her eyes. But Ana smiled at Tony's silly joke, too. There really wasn't much more for them to do.

"I guess let's just sleep on it," Ana said. "And we'll figure out the rest of our lives…tomorrow."

"Sure," Val said, though she didn't sound convinced.

While they would have loved nothing more than to wind down and sleep in their own homes, they said goodnight and went their separate ways.

No one minded the few droplets of rain that began to fall as they made their own ways home. They hardly even balked at the lightning, but when thunder boomed across the sky, they were all happy to get into safe, warm homes, no matter whose they were.

They'd all lost power at some point, but they were far too tired to care. All four of them took themselves to bed as soon as they could, welcoming sleep as a gentle reprieve from the hectic day they'd had.

*     *     *

When Tony woke up in the morning, the first thing he noticed was the way the light hit his Dungeons & Dragons poster. He jumped out of bed, delighted to find himself in his own room, his clothes, his *body*. After quickly changing into proper pants and a t-shirt, he bolted out of his room, down the stairs and past the kitchen.

He'd almost made it to the front door when Maddy called out to him, "Hey, what's up? Did you want something to eat or...do you need anything?"

Now was not the time for him to be doted on, but he didn't want to be rude. So, he gently said, "Later, Mads. I got a girl to see. Sorry."

Her eyebrows lifted and she said in a surprised voice, "Tony?"

"Yes?" he said impatiently.

"Nothing." She smiled. "Have a good time with that girl."

"Uh huh."

Finally, he was free, and he raced out the door. But after a minute, he realized what Ana meant when she'd said his body wasn't built for running. He stopped, took a deep breath, and forced himself to calm down. It was hard to do when all he wanted to do was see Ana, *as* Ana.

Instead of running, he walked at the fastest pace he could tolerate. His phone started ringing as soon as he got to Ana's street and he answered it without even looking, thinking it was probably Sam.

"Tony!"

Now that was Ana's beautiful voice. "Hey."

"I'm me!"

He chuckled. "Me, too."

"Where are you?"

"Literally, down the street from your house."

"You...you are?" She sounded so surprised he almost laughed again. "Okay, hold on, I'll be right there."

Tony stopped and took another deep breath, this time to calm his racing heart. Sure, he'd wanted to see Ana desperately. But now that she was coming to him what was he supposed to say or do?

He didn't have time to think about it as she came rushing down the street in the same pyjamas he'd put on last night. The ones with the soft pink flannel pants and t-shirt with a big heart on it. She'd thrown her hair up into a messy bun, and his heart pounded even harder at the huge smile she gave him.

"Look at you," she said as she gently grasped his elbows.

"No, look at *you*," he said, pulling her a few inches forward. "You're so...cute!"

Her cheeks went pink as she laughed. Then she got a little lost in his eyes for a moment while they stood still. It was so much nicer to look into those eyes than through them.

"Okay, I'm just gonna do it." She leaned into him, wrapping her arms around his neck as his face leaned towards hers. That was far better than the first—and second—time they'd kissed. "See?" she whispered after she'd pulled back. "Not that complicated."

"I definitely don't hate that at all." He started to dip his head again but stopped when his phone rang. Gently extricating himself from her, he hastily grabbed his phone, and his eyes lit up. "Sam!"

"Tony?"

"Yeah, it's me, man."

"Oh, good." Sam let out a long sigh. "Me, too. Where are you? We gotta do something fun."

"Oh, I—" Tony looked at Ana, who smiled softly at him. "I'm...with Ana. Just making sure she's okay."

"Oh." Sam paused a moment. "Of course. Is she?"

"Yeah."

"Okay, I'll see you later then."

"No, well—" Tony didn't want Sam to feel left out. He should have checked on Sam first, now that he thought about it. "Well, why don't you call Val, and we can all hang out?"

"Um...yeah, I'll see. Text you later?"

"Yeah."

Tony hung up and looked back at Ana, who asked if Sam and Val had also switched back, too. Tony nodded. "You were right. All we needed was to sleep on it."

"I'm right a lot," she teased. "So are we hanging out with them?"

Tony hesitated. He and Sam were together all the time. But Ana was here right now, not rejecting him even after the strange situation they'd just been in. "Maybe later."

"Breakfast, then?" She held out her hand and he didn't have to think twice about taking it. Breakfast with Ana sounded far better than breakfast *as* Ana.

*     *     *

Sam lowered his phone, trying not to be disappointed that Tony had chosen Ana over him. After all, Sam had many times decided to hang out with a girl instead of Tony. It was Tony's turn to have that privilege. In fact, if he thought Val would ever want to see him again, he would be doing the same thing Tony was.

Instead, he stared at Val's number in his phone for a minute. Girls could call boys. They had every right. Maybe she was about to do that. Or maybe she was glad to be rid of Sam until the end of time.

Figuring he should at least make sure she was okay, he texted, "You good?" and cringed as soon as he'd hit Send. That was, by far, the worst text he'd ever sent a girl. And of course all she sent back was a thumbs up emoji. Perfect. He'd successfully quashed any semblance of a tenable relationship with her.

Sighing, he left his bedroom, comforted by the smell of freshly brewed coffee. Following his nose, he found Ty in the kitchen, already pouring himself a cup.

"Hey, can I have some of that?" Sam asked, forcing the words past the lump in his throat.

Ty turned to him with a surprised look. "You…want coffee today?"

217

"Yes," Sam said wearily as he sat at the table. "Please. Like I always take it."

"Oh!" Ty grabbed the creamer that had been sitting untouched in the fridge for the past week. He usually drank his coffee black and only ever bought flavoured creamers for Sam. He brought the cup over to Sam.

As Sam wrapped his hand around the mug, he said, "You're the best brother in the whole wide world.

Ty smiled and sat across from him. "I'm happy to have you around, Sam."

"Me, too."

# Chapter Twenty-Eight

Val had woken up to the sound of buzzing in her ear. A phone, she assumed, letting her know that once again, someone needed her attention. In the distance, Juliette and Harrison were singing a duet wildly out of tune and raucously enough that Val was surprised they hadn't woken her before the phone.

Then she sat up straight in bed. *Her* bed! She was back in her own body in a set of silk pyjamas she never would have worn that Sam clearly hadn't been able to resist.

Sam!

She got the phone and discovered it was him who had texted. Two words. She couldn't blame him, she supposed. He probably didn't send long lengthy texts about how even though they'd just gone through a terrifying—and yet somehow not entirely awful—experience together, he still wanted to see her and spend time with her. And since he wasn't going to, she wouldn't either, because she didn't want to be the first one to say it. In fact, she would only send him an emoji. He would get the idea.

Then she burst out of her room and went out to Harrison's room where the concert was still ongoing. "You guys sound awful. Let me sing the melody."

They laughed and let her join in. And even though the song was worse now, Val wouldn't trade this for the world. Not even for another photoshoot as a hot male model. No, she would take this.

Halfway through the song, Shadow found them and immediately jumped up on her, attempting to knock her over so he could sit in her lap. He was too big for it, and she knew she shouldn't let him bowl her over like that. But she'd missed him so much that she nearly cried when he licked her face.

Everything was as it should be. She was back to herself and so was Sam. They could go back to their own lives and back to pretending the other didn't exist. Wonderful.

She did give a second thought to Ana and Tony and so she texted Ana quickly to ask. Yes, they had switched back. Tony had immediately gone over to her house to see if what they felt in each other's bodies would stay the same in their own. It had.

This confirmed that Sam hadn't felt a single thing for Val while they were swapped, other than contempt and distaste. And that was fine with Val. She'd lived her whole life without him and she could continue to live her life alone.

*     *     *

*1 week later*

It was a beautiful Sunday morning, and the sun beat down on Tony. Thankfully, he'd remembered a hat today. He turned the ball in his glove before raising his hand. He lobbed a hard and fast one straight towards Ana, who didn't quite swing quickly enough to hit it. He grinned and she rolled her eyes as she went to retrieve it.

"Wow, you're really getting good at this, T."

She tossed the ball back to him and he caught it easily. "Yeah, I had a good teacher."

She smirked. "Okay, great, but can you not try to strike me out this time?"

"No promises." Despite his joke, Tony threw her a slightly easier pitch, which she hit with incredibly weight.

He whistled as he followed the ball's path in a beautiful arc across the field. "Wowie, Ana. I mean, Sarah would have definitely caught that, but since it's just me and you, you should run the bases."

She laughed, tossed her bat aside, and jogged around the diamond. It wasn't necessary, but it did feel nice when he met her at home plate with his arms open wide. She rested her head on his shoulder as he squeezed her tight.

"I could stay like this forever," he murmured into her hair.

"Okay, but you said I could practice pitching on you, too, so..." She pulled back, kissed him quickly, and nodded towards where she'd hit the ball.

Shaking his head and smiling, he ran to get it. As she'd requested, they practiced for a little while longer. Tony was way worse at batting than he was at pitching, especially when Ana was pitching for him. But neither of them minded. They just enjoyed the time together.

When she decided it was time for a break, they sat on the pitcher's mound together, facing each other and holding hands. She had a defined frown on her face, and even a kiss on each of her hands couldn't turn it upside down.

"What's wrong?" he asked.

"Are Val and Sam still not talking to each other?"

Tony shrugged to try to cover up how disappointed he felt for Sam. "I tried talking to him, but he just changes the subject. I think he thinks she'll reject him if he even tries to get close."

Ana sighed. "She likes him! I mean, she doesn't ever say it, but it's obvious."

"She's always staring."

"Except when he's looking, of course."

"Of course. And he's totally into her. But, you know, without being *in* her body."

Ana giggled. "We have to do something. But I think I have a plan."

He smiled with her. "Let's hear it!"

*      *      *

Sam walked into his favourite ice cream shop and took a big whiff. It always smelled like vanilla and strawberry sauce and freshly made cones, so when Tony had invited him to go on a whim, Sam had jumped at the chance. He hadn't been there in a long time and was looking forward to binging something he rarely had at home.

A quick glance around told him Tony hadn't arrived yet. However, Sam did see a very familiar pair of dark brown eyes tracking him. The same pair that never seemed to leave him at school, even though Val had barely said a word to him since they'd gotten their own bodies back.

But now a smile accompanied the glint in her eyes, and she waved. He waved back and, feeling encouraged, went over to the red and white checkered table she sat at.

"Hey," he said.

"Hi," she said with warmth in her voice. "Are you also here to meet someone who's clearly not coming?"

Sam lifted an eyebrow and glanced at the door. The bell above it would have signaled his friend's entrance. Shaking his head, he sat across from Val. "Seems like it, yeah. Did we get set up?"

"I think so." Val's smile widened as she gestured to the order counter. "If you tell me your favourite flavour, I'll get you a cone."

Sam smiled back. After a whole week of her silence, he'd take anything from her. "Pistachio."

"Get out," she said as she rose. "I love pistachio! Give me two minutes."

Val took a deep breath as she went to the counter. She finally had Sam all to herself thanks to Ana and Tony's sneakiness. Maybe if she was smart—

which she generally was—she wouldn't mess this up. Maybe she could even tell Sam she missed him, despite never wanting to live in his body again.

She ordered two cones of pistachio ice cream and when she brought them back, she nearly tripped over her own feet at the smile he gave her. Had he missed her, too? She shoved the ice cream at him and turned away as he began eating it. She could barely look at him without knowing how he felt about her.

When they'd gotten about halfway through their treats, he asked, "So, how have you been? I haven't…had a chance to ask yet."

"I'm good, Sam," she said softly. "Juliette showed me a video from the debate. She said it was my best one yet and…she wasn't wrong. You were great."

He smiled. "I tried my best. Sorry I took that dig at Daniel."

"Don't be. He deserved it. He wins all the debates. But I see now how being a little more charismatic like you can win people over." She took another few licks of her ice cream. "How are you doing?"

"I'm good." It was only half a lie. "Oh! The photographer sent me some of the photos already. He said he loved taking my picture so much he couldn't wait to start editing."

"Really?"

"Yeah, check these out."

He pulled out his phone, opened up the specially saved folder, and passed the phone to her. Her heart skipped a beat when she saw the first one. It was from the very moment when Gill had told her to think of her crush and smile. She'd thought of Sam, and she could see how her smile on his face could light up any picture.

"You were right about the smiling," Sam said. "Gill told me that was his favourite pose. The others are good, too, but he says that one was the best. You did a great job."

She swiped some more. They *all* looked good. "I know I was the one there, but these are pictures of *you*, Sam. You're the one who picks the clothes, and the looks, and keeps himself looking good. All I did was…follow the instructions. I'm good at *that*."

Leaning in, Sam bobbed his eyebrows and said, "I bet if he got *you* into the studio, he'd make you look magical, too."

"Stop," she mumbled as heat rose to her cheeks. She dropped her gaze, the last little bit of her cone forgotten in her hand.

"Val."

When she flicked her gaze back up, she found him quite a bit more serious than before. "Sam?"

He licked his lips and leaned in even further. "I miss you."

Her breath caught in her throat. "Me, too," she whispered.

"I didn't think you…" He let his sentence trail off but kept his eyes on her.

"Didn't think I what?" she prompted.

"I didn't think you'd ever want to see me again," he said. "I'm just some dumb guy who really doesn't fit into your world."

"That's not true."

"It is. But that's okay."

"Sam."

"No, it's okay."

"Stop." Feeling uncommonly impulsive, she put her hand on the side of his face and pulled him close enough to kiss. He tasted like pistachio ice cream and promises, and his lips were soft and inviting. If she could bottle this feeling, she'd make a killing.

"*Val*," he whispered against her lips.

"I know. I've never done anything like that."

"I'm totally okay with it."

Chuckling, she pulled back. Pointing to his hand, she said, "Your ice cream is melting all over the place."

"Like my *heart*."

"Wow." She rolled her eyes, though truthfully, her heart a melted a little too.

Sam laughed as he attempted to clean his hand off. "So, what are you doing after this?"

"Nothing," she said, opening the door a little wider. "Absolutely nothing."

"Oh, good. Tony and Ana were going to come over after and have dinner with me and Ty and Maddy." Sam smirked. "And I don't want to be a fifth wheel tonight. You want to come?"

"Yes."

"You didn't even think about it."

"I didn't have to. You could have asked me to do anything, and I would have said yes."

Sam's entire body filled with warmth. Quickly, he finished what was left of his ice cream while she did the same. When they were done, he offered her his hand, which she took without hesitation.

On the way, Sam called Tony, berated him for being sneaky, thanked him for his sneakiness, and then told him he was still invited over. At the apartment, Ty and Maddy were goofing off in the kitchen and "cooking" the meal. When Ty saw Val, he nodded at her in a familiar way. Sam chose not to comment.

Ana and Tony joined them a few minutes later, and eventually the food was finished cooking. They sat around the table and passed out all the sides Maddy had made.

Maddy was just about to take her first bite when Ty said, "So, did you four get yourselves sorted out or what?"

Maddy elbowed him hard while Sam and Tony gave each other startled looks across the table. Tony said, "Okay, who told?"

Sheepishly, Ana raised her hand followed by Val. The boys rolled their eyes.

Maddy said, "And then I told him—" She swatted Ty's chest.

"And I told her back." Ty's eyes twinkled with laughter he was holding back. "That was the most entertaining week of my life."

"Same," Maddy said happily.

Tony put his head in his hands and groaned while Ana patted his back. But Sam laughed as he put his arm around Val's shoulders. Entertaining or not, it was a week they wouldn't soon forget.

## A NOTE FROM THE AUTHOR

Thank you so much for reading my book! If this is your first of my body swappers, you're in for a delicious treat. If you've read the rest of the Swapped Lives series, try one of my other series! I've got lots to pick from.

If you loved this book and want to see more from me, why not follow my newsletter for monthly updates? Sign up here and get a free story right away! https://www.subscribepage.com/natasjaeby

—Natasja ♥

# THE SWAPPED LIVES SERIES

# OTHER SERIES BY NATASJA EBY

# ABOUT THE AUTHOR

Natasja is a librarian and the self-published author of the Swapped Lives series, the Knockout Girl series, the Onepian Chronicles, and the Less than Perfect series. She is an avid fan and participant of NaNoWriMo and has completed several novels over the past few Novembers.

In 2019, Natasja received two Indie Original awards for *Knockout Girl*, one for Best New Author and the other for Best Young Adult Novel.

When she's not working on her many unfinished novels, she can be found playing video games with her husband and two kids, singing, or curled up with a good book. Natasja lives just outside of Toronto—close enough for good shopping and far enough to avoid the traffic.

Follow her on social media!
https://www.natasjaeby.com/
https://www.facebook.com/Natasja.Eby/
https://www.instagram.com/natasjaeby/
https://twitter.com/NatasjaEby